HAPPYLAND

HAPPYLAND

A Story
by

ALAN WYKES

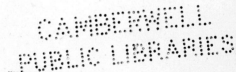

GERALD DUCKWORTH & CO. LTD.
3 HENRIETTA STREET, LONDON, W.C.2

First published 1952

Set in 11 pt. Intertype Baskerville, 1 pt. leaded and printed in Great
Britain by the Bristol Typesetting Company, Stokes Croft, Bristol

TO
MY FATHER AND MOTHER
WITH LOVE

The visitor from the distant planet then said to the philosophers: "O intelligent creatures, in whom God has been pleased to manifest his ability and his power, doubtless you taste the greatest of joys upon your globe. I have found happiness nowhere else: doubtless it is to be found here."

The senior philosopher, who chanced also to be the most honest, replied: "Except for a small number of people, held to be of little account, everyone on earth is either mad, sinful, or greatly miserable."

"Then tell me of the small number held to be of little account," the visitor said.

VOLTAIRE *Micromégas.*

I

At Manor House tube station the trains came in every few seconds. The crowds came off them, moving slowly, solidly, toward the escalators. *Harringay Arena* the luminous posters said, *Tschaikowski Concert;* and, interspersed with these, *Dogs. Have the Biggest Bet of your Life with Angus Toole.*

There were arrows for music and arrows for dogs, no fear of confusion. At the top were the labyrinthine blue and yellow corridors, the dirt car park, the patent fire extinguishers, the commissionaires with white hats calling "Music this way. This way"—repetitively raucous on the chill and hospitalised spring dusk. "Music this way."

At the entrance to the arena Harold Bassett bought an *Evening Standard.* With a faintly contemptuous glance at its front page he folded the paper in *Tribune,* which he already carried tucked under his arm. The same arm was draped with a folded raincoat. The raincoat had been dry-cleaned and was now unnaturally light in colour, but was already beginning to show new streaks of grime in its folds. Since he had come straight from the Soho gramophone shop where he worked he wore his blue suit. It was serge, beginning to gloss a little, carefully pressed. He fussed about sartorial matters and it irked him to have his ties and socks unmatching and the handkerchief in his breast pocket too obtrusive. He believed that he hated both vulgarity and sentimentality; and sometimes he smiled with tolerant amusement when his girl, Doris Cheeseman, admitted to a liking for the *Zampa* overture or the cheaper women's magazines or ginger wine. His own tastes ran to Tschai-

7

kowski and Rachmaninoff, French films, pink gins. He was trying to raise Doris's taste without being too obvious about it, for he liked to consider other people's feelings.

He had Doris with him now. He shepherded her forward, his free hand lightly at her elbow. She was a slim blonde girl with carefully styled hair (she worked in a hairdresser's) and good legs. She was hatless, but wore a camelhair coat, belted tightly.

They both had the look of people who are inwardly sustained by some tremendous secret compulsion, a conspiratorial air both revolutionary and diabolic, aimed with a kind of smug virulence at what they thought of as ' petty conventions.' They had in fact for some time now been considering, even planning, an elopement.

There was no real need for them to elope, since they were both of age and their parents had expressed none but trivial words of opposition; but the thought was exciting, it outraged respectability, and the vague idea stirred somewhere in their imagination that such a course, backed by the necessary courage, would ensure happiness because it was an act of individual will that had to be made and sustained.

After the concert they came unhurriedly out of the arena. "No point in getting crushed to death by the masses," Harold Bassett said. He had his pipe in his mouth, and again he shepherded Doris forward with a chummy touch at her elbow. He paused to light his pipe, and in the matchglow Doris saw his face with an inward personal vision which, had she considered it at all, she would have thought of rather coyly as adoration.

The crowd had thinned by the time they reached the platform and when the train came in they were able to get seats. "You might just as well as comfortable," Doris said. She was unaware how often she echoed Harold's words;

but if the thought had occurred to her it would have been with approval. She constantly felt a faint and inexplicable disgust with emancipated women. To her femininity meant the acknowledgment of male mastery; but she was careful to disguise this, for it would have been dreadful to be ' old fashioned.' Somehow, obscurely, it would have been letting Harold down.

Harold turned to her. His light, almost putty coloured eyes regarded her with approval. " All right?" He meant the concert.

" Lovely." She sensed at once that he disapproved of the word in connection with such a serious thing as music, just as she sensed his disapproval of her making any public demonstration of affection such as linking one of her fingers with his; but there was constant and irrevocable compensation in the knowledge that he had once admitted " I can't ever get you out of my mind as I first saw you." In a tiny pigeonhole in his mind was tucked away an image of her, cherished and unsullied. She was wearing the pink linen overall with the short sleeves and the tied sash and the combs and scissors of her trade protruding from the pocket across which was embroidered in black, *Doris*. Yes, she was there in his mind all right : sometimes he thought of her high breasts and the line of her throat and her waist that he could encircle with his two hands : she knew he did and it made her pensively happy.

He spread the evening paper on his knees. The face of a middle-aged clerk or floorwalker headed a half-column story on the front page. *Mr. Mountalban pictured at his Mayfair desk.* Mr. Mountalban's hair was thinning and his clothes were neat. One would have said he had a tidy little garden and a wife who went to whist drives; but his story was headlined :

9

WHAT IS HAPPYLAND?

*Mr. Eric Mountalban, chief of Mountalban Invest-
ments Corporation, controllers of a score of big-busi-
ness enterprises, said at a press conference today: 'I
am floating my new £2 million company Happyland
Ltd., for the potential good of every man, woman and
child in this country. As soon as the necessary formalities are completed I shall be offering the general public
a facility that has never before been available to them
anywhere in the world.'*

*Pressed for further details and questioned about the
significance of the new company's name, Mr. Mountalban said: 'I am not yet at liberty to disclose details.
To do so would mean heavy over-subscription when
the new flotation is made. You can infer what significance you like from the name.'*

*Asked 'Is Happyland a holiday camp?' he replied
decisively, 'Definitely no. Others are interested in
holiday camps. I am not.'*

At the foot of the stop press column was another brief
paragraph :

HAPPYLAND (See this page)

*Tom Prospect, the Holiday Camp King, who runs
the 'Prospect-Before-You' camps round Britain's
coast, said today: 'The only new word in holiday
camps is Elysium. It's the name of the new one I'm
building on the north-east coast. I don't know anything about any Happyland. It sounds crazy to me.'*

Doris said : " What's it all mean?"

"Some twaddle. Who cares?"

She sat composed and silent. After a while she said: "Happyland. There is a happy land, far, far away. D'you think that's it: some kind of religious thing?"

Harold Bassett took the pipe from his mouth. "I wouldn't know." But the word was beginning to groove his mind. Happyland. He felt as he always felt after a concert: nauseated with the world of triviality you returned to from the world of sound. Happyland: stupidly he was letting the word connect in some way with the surreptitious and as yet formless plan for their elopement; and as the train roared again into a tunnel he saw in the dark-slanted glass opposite that Doris was looking excited too.

"Happyland," she murmured. "There's something nice about it somehow"; and, fumbling with the phrasing of an elusive thought: "Something for us—somehow."

It was almost frightening that it should occur to her too. Whatever it was he disposed of it the easy way; taking the pipe from his mouth he said with tolerant amusement: "How do you mean—'somehow'?"

At the next station they changed to another line. It was at this stage of the journey that they began to think of their homes—a kind of automatic resumption of thought brought about as it were by simple physical proximity. They liked to imagine that the terraced houses and the backyards and the pigeons and the schoolgirl sister and the palpable re-iterated boredom of daily conventionalities extended their net over a certain area, that outside that area they were free.

At first, in the days when they had only known each other, had decided nothing, it had been a kind of link that had grown stronger each time one of them said: "What a ghastly bind it is—going home and all that."

Then, after a while, without any word having actually

been spoken, the idea of revolution somehow became a real thing : it was framed in the derisive words they tacked round the evoked picture of the pettiness of home life. There was nothing for them but to deride : only in that way could they be sure of themselves.

The parents of both of them were respectable people living at opposite ends of the town in houses essentially alike. Mr. Bassett was a draper and a Buffalo. He had worked in the same shop for an inadequate wage which he never questioned, or even thought of questioning, for thirty years. He and his wife were both middle-aged when Harold was born. There had been two other children—both boys. The eldest, Arthur, had secured a position in the same draper's shop as the father. It was a shop in the old part of the town, sited on a corner, with a fascia of dull red glass in which the gold letters were cut, and windows in which combinations and yellow dusters and reels of ribbon and dateless and ageless millinery hung and stood and protruded as in the airing room of an ancient laundry. The other son, Basil, as befitted his name and conspicuous superiority, had gone into a solicitor's office.

Harold despised both his brothers. His father he merely thought stupid. For his mother he had an odd weak affection, and sometimes he almost believed that she had depth of character.

His upbringing was extremely strict. The very fact of his father's daily unending routine of journeys to and from the shop and, once a week, to the greenwalled hall where the Buffalo met, imposed on the life of the entire household an unflagging mechanisation that was quite impossible to disrupt.

Gradually the boy learned to despise this too; but since nothing would have been gained and everything lost by disclosure of the fact, he kept his contempt to himself. He was conscious of struggling to climb out of a morass of vulgarity more deadly than poison. Day by day he read and watched and listened to the opinions of others. He was quite sure that they were his own opinions that were developing.

The parents left him alone, a little puzzled and a little proud of his acquired taste and knowledge. Arthur was steady and reliable, Basil was bright with his answers and quick at figures, Harold was a bit of a mystery with his music and his strange books and his periodicals that, being being simple people themselves, they never suspected he left lying about opened at pages heavy with obscure learning. They were happy. " He'll go a long way, that boy," Mr. Bassett said. He spoke with brooding significance, a habit that had come upon him with years of attention to the customers he served—the same tranquil women day after day with their pensive devotion to modes and qualities long forgotten in newer and smarter shops.

" He'll do," his wife said.

The Cheesman family might have been cast in the same imperturbable and unheroic mould. The parents had been married at eighteen and within a year their first child, a boy, had been born and died. A year later another boy was born. He also died. Mrs. Cheesman set her face at these two losses with an acceptance that was not so much indomitable as superstitious. " We won't ever rear boys. I'm certain of it." She felt so certain that when another boy was born and went on living she felt an obscure resentment. Aware somehow that such resentment was wicked and against the will of God, she lavished every devotion and care on the child by way of atonement. He lived to be six years old and then died of meningitis. After his death she felt quieter, happier, as if her sin had been expiated.

She was thirty when Doris was born; and nine years

after that came Daphne. She had no fears about either of her daughters. She had been destined, she knew, to bear and rear girl children and here at last they were.

They were good girls. The father was earning a fair wage as a compositor in a small printing works that printed posters, billheads, visiting cards and the like, and he was able to lay down ten pounds, which was to be repaid as pocket money at five shillings a week, for Doris's apprenticeship to a hairdresser named Bunce. He knew nothing of Bunce beyond the fact that he was a middle-aged and respected business man.

Doris went there when she was sixteen. By the time two years had passed she was a qualified hairdresser with a diploma to which was affixed a gold seal on which her name was inscribed in a lavish copperplate handwriting. The diploma was framed and stood in the window of Bunce's shop, backed by black velvet curtains hanging on brass rings and flanked by lithographed showcards and pots of face cream and manicure requisites. Occasionally, when she was out shopping, Mrs. Cheeseman made surreptitious journeys past the window so that she could look at the diploma with wonder.

One night when Doris was nineteen she was at the shop rather later than usual. She had been giving a customer a permanent wave and the other two assistants had gone.

Bunce was in the office behind the shop and when the customer had at last gone Doris called in at the door:

" I'll be off now then, Mr. Bunce."

He turned in his chair and looked at her. He was a blue-eyed gentle man of fifty or so. Now, as he looked at Doris, she was astonished to see his eyes filled with tears.

" You're so very beautiful," he said. " So very beautiful."

He said nothing else, and he made no move to touch her or even come near her. She felt flushed and a little embarrassed and sensuously disturbed. She believed she had an inkling of what he was going through and she felt a quick and complex pity for him. She said with elaborate casualness: "Thanks, awfully." And after a pause: "Well, I'll say goodnight, then."

After she had left the shop she was shocked to discover that even as she walked quickly away down the High Street she was wondering whether or not she should return on some pretext and ask him what was wrong, perhaps touch his forehead with her hand.

She told no one of the incident and it was never repeated. In fact sometimes she wondered whether she had imagined it. But from that time forward she felt she was completely adult, that beyond the horizons of terrace houses and concrete backyards there lay a real, if unattainable, excitement.

When she met Harold Bassett (he had become acquainted with her simply by stationing himself on four successive Saturdays outside Bunce's shop in a position and attitude nicely calculated to imply that he had only to be acknowledged to be known, should she wish it) she became immediately aware that the unattainable was in fact nothing more than that which needed a little more will-power, a shifting of the viewpoint, an understanding. What she had lacked was a guide, someone who had the daring to call a spade a spade, to commiserate with her when she had to stay in to keep an eye on Daphne on the regular weekly occasions when, regardless of the film, her parents visited the Regal, but at the same time to inaugurate in her mind an idea: the idea of breaking away.

"Else it'll go on for ever."

Puzzled, she asked him: "You mean we ought to get married?"

Carefully taking the pipe from his mouth so that she

could see he was serious he answered: "Provided you get your attitude to marriage right first. There's nothing against it, but you've got to realise that if it's going to lead to the same life we're trying to escape, then it's nothing but legalised—well, intercourse."

So what they sought thereafter—Doris seeking it because Harold in his respected mastery and masculine understanding bade her or perhaps just made it appear idealised enough for her to want to seek it; and Harold himself seeking it because only the projection of some glamorised and cerebrally emotional idea seemed to have real substance after the despised ordinances and pettifoggery that palled the twenty years of his life he had so far lived—was an adventurous undertone to which they could listen secretly and with a kind of lustful avarice at once humble and utopian, that they could at least long for or worship or perhaps simply believe existed, so that on some dimly apprehended future morning they could look at each other and without speaking know that something was indeed sounding—something brave and new and inspired.

After a while it became something not simply indulged in but lived—a separate existence altogether into which they could plunge whenever they were together; not simply something revolutionary to think of but an El Dorado to which they could make their way via the acquisition of taste and what Harold thought of as culture, and secret and illimitably funny gibes at the life of suburban conventionality they had been forced to endure by accident of birth. They were brightly thankful that they had seen the danger in time, that they themselves would never repeat the awful dulness of their parents' lives.

But symbolically, for the time being, the return home had to be made, the net of conventionality and fatuous conversation had to be endured for a while; and each time

16

they reached, say, Charing Cross, after an evening out they implied by looks what they had long since ceased to state in words:

" What a bind—going home."

On this night of the Tschaikowski concert they saw by chance someone who, though they were never to know it, by just such another chance encounter and the subsequent action he knew it was his duty as well as his pleasure to take, had already set his mark upon their lives.

They passed him on the escalator—a sallow-skinned man in decorous and unobtrusive black clothes, his ears large, his spectacles thick, his manner decent and professorial.

He was going down and Harold and Doris were going up. At the point where they drew level Harold chanced to turn and saw him. He took his pipe from his mouth and acknowledged him with what he called his ' shop ' smile. The other responded vaguely, his hand before his mouth in a sudden spasm of indigestion. And then they were past each other. That was all.

" Who's the old boy?" Doris said.

They reached the top. With his fingers beneath her elbow he guided her lightly off the escalator. " A customer. He buys old mechanical recordings—Clara Butt, Pachmann, people like that. Hopeless type. Dim, dotty, always hiccoughing and taking soda tablets. Birch, his name is. Or, Bitch—is it Bitch?"

" I wouldn't know."

" Why should you? I haven't told you yet. I'll get it in a minute."

They walked from the station up Villiers Street. A cold May wind blew down past the restaurants and the barrows. On the railings of the gardens the posters advertising the band concerts were streaky in the lamp-light. " Fitch," he said suddenly. " That's it—Fitch. Got a flat in Bloomsbury.

17

He's just the tatty type who would have." Musing, he said :
" Fitch. The son of a bitch," and waited for Doris to laugh,
to say, ' Oh, you are a one '—dragging up the phrase from
a life that held them with the tenacity of faith, a faith that
could be clung to and hated too.

II

ONE afternoon in winter Fitch had come to Mr. Mountalban bringing information.

Fitch was a man who was paid to listen. With his dormant stomach ulcer and his catalogue of rare gramophone
records he could stow himself unobtrusively away in any
odd corner and no one would bother him. He was a silent,
rubber-soled man who exemplified that quality of insigni-
ficance essential to the professional eavesdropper. Years of
practise had perfected in him the art of merging into the
background. He was left alone with his thick glasses and his
pocket container of bismuth tablets. It was a solitude he
never resented : in a way he was proud of it—it was satisfying to be able to earn so much by doing so little. Mr.
Mountalban paid Fitch well; and Fitch had proved his
worth many times.

He possessed not only a genius for happening to be
within easy hearing of countless things that didn't concern
him, but, vastly more important, a genius for recognising
truth and significance—the truth insofar as it was the
motivation of whispered confidences, and the significance
as it would affect Mr. Mountalban and, ultimately, himself.

Small things first : he had heard much that was useful
among the guarded, guided, unguarded and misguided

conversations in trains and bars and parks. Later, Mr. Mountalban having acknowledged his worth, he had bigger and better opportunities: social, diplomatic and financial circles were most fruitful, and one February day in Cradle's Club, to which Mr. Mountalban was remotely responsible for Fitch's admission, he sensed the biggest opportunity of all.

That day Fitch ate at noon. He had four dry biscuits and a glass of hot water into which he unobtrusively dropped a bismuth tablet. He then went into the smoking room, sat in an armchair before the fire, opened the Soho dealer's catalogue of rare and historic gramophone records, and waited, listening.

Amid the incumbent and desiccated atmosphere of the smoking room the single genteel waiter hovered soundlessly. On the walls the hunting scenes and Spy drawings of men in garb redolent of an age long gone yet curiously apposite in time and place, as though they were the founder members of the club and had by precept and example set the tone that was by rote adhered to, were bloomed with a thin film of something less than dirt—something that was indefinably present as it were in the very air of each high-and carved-ceilinged room, a thin and toneless and epicene grandeur that remained helplessly untouched by the fall of empires and civilisations.

The waiter hovered. A few members came and went, glancing at the journals in their embossed leather covers, sitting in the heavy armchairs, conversing in secret and mumbling undertones. Fitch, sitting with his eyes closed, could hear them all. There was nothing worth hearing. A few strands of conversation might conceivably have been of use to a blackmailer, but Fitch certainly was not that: his stomach would never have stood the strain of a conscience. He could also observe perfectly well; from time to time he would allow his eyelids to part, gently and unobtrusively, and his glance to stray with the same unobtrusive skill to whoever was within its ken and to the massive mirrored overmantel above the fireplace.

It was in the mirror that he saw the Earl enter the smoking room accompanied, shepherded, by Drew. Of Drew Fitch took no notice at all, beyond remarking that his presence heralded an introduction. Drew was a member of the club, a classicist of distinction, whom Fitch had never known to engage in any act of direct consequence other than the introduction of two strangers to each other. He was, as it were, a passive link in a chain of human relationships, a kind of mechanical Debrett who performed his minor duty and departed. But the Earl was of immediate interest to Fitch.

Although at that moment Fitch knew nothing of him beyond what he could see for himself of stature and age and dress, not even his rank or name, though both were to be familiar to him so soon as he heard them, he sensed the importance of what he called one of his hunches. He was sensitive to coming disclosures as a water diviner is sensitive to the presence of water. He had evolved for himself what he fancied to be a literary style of thought and with harmless glee he imagined himself ' responding with every fibre of his being ' to the happy occasion of disclosure and confidence.

This was one of the occasions. He was certain—certain.

Drew and the Earl crossed the room and most happily chose a sofa that backed onto Fitch's armchair. Fitch slid deeper into the chair. In the mirror he saw the two men sit down. The Earl was old and lean and firm-fleshed; he looked not jovial but happy. The lean classical face was unravaged by any kind of sorrow; it was as if all his life he had remained static in the presence of an untroubled

20

childhood. His hair was short and straight and upended, like a worn shaving brush. On the narrow tough body was draped a mud-coloured suit in a style of forty or more years ago—the coat long-skirted and centre-vented and with cuffs to the sleeves. In the high narrow lapel was a cream rose on a triolet of leaves.

" The Minister will be here in a moment," Drew said in his soft scholar's voice. He seemed to sense that his own significance was akin to that of a jester in an Elizabethan tragedy. His eyes had the contented look of a loved dog.

" Yes," the Earl said. He seemed to muse on what he was about to say. " There is ample time—ample."

" Of course it would seem so to you," Drew said gravely. " Ah, here is the Minister."

The Minister now entered and crossed the room—a man well aware of his public charm, his hand lying with down-pointed fingers on his hip as he walked, catching back the sombrely yet exquisitely cut black jacket to display the grey double-breasted waistcoat and the monocle on its thin cord, the manner rhetorical and histrionic, the thin straight lips parted on slightly malformed teeth, the sparse black hair arranged in carefully polished segments. " This is a happy occasion," he said.

Drew introduced the Minister to the Earl. With unaffected formality he spoke their names and rank. When Fitch heard the Earl's name he thought of it as it appeared in the pages of Burke and Debrett—the unusually simple statement of lineage and establishment and residence, unamplified by details of accomplishment or heirs or heraldry, occupying perhaps ten lines of print and those almost humble, apologetic. ' So that's him,' Fitch thought.

" I'll leave you," Drew said.

" Have a drink before you go," the Minister said. " A toast—to success."

21

" Thank you—no," Drew said, his voice still grave, gentle, perhaps even mildly reproachful. " Though I wish you success nonetheless." He went out.

" A neutral man," the Minister said. " Neutral. Negligible. Average. Dull." His elocutionary voice mused over the words. " Sensationally mediocre. Waiter, bring two ports —no, on consideration bring a bottle. This is an occasion. A national occasion." When the waiter had brought the port he added with oratorical deliberation : " We might even say an international occasion."

" I suppose it might even become that." The Earl spoke with gentle courtesy. " I understand that you, I mean His Majesty's Government, are interested in buying my island home."

" If you're interested in selling, yes—I think I can safely say yes."

The Earl sipped his port. Once, between sips, he lifted his lapel and bent his nose to the scent of the rose. " It seems so long since I cut it; yet it was only yesterday morning."

" I shall need a few details," the Minister said.

" Of course. It's difficult to explain, to make convincing. But I must do my best."

" Size," the Minister said. " Population—we shall need to know what arrangements we must make for evacuation. Price. Those are the three main considerations."

In the mirror Fitch saw the Earl's fine-boned feudal profile turned toward the Minister. " Evacuation? Size?" he said with the same gentle courtesy to which was now added a slight and puzzled amusement; " I think I shall have to tell you rather more than that."

The Minister carefully masked his impatience. " I'm seeing the C.I.G.S. at four."

The Earl's head bent again to the rose. " The C.I.G.S.? He's a General, isn't he? A soldier of some kind?"

"Yes, yes. Actually a Field-Marshal. He's the most interested party, of course."

"I had not thought of soldiers understanding happiness particularly. However—"

"Happiness?" the Minister said; and again, "Happiness?" His voice was level, glossing his impatience with something of contemptuous amusement. "You realise of course that what we want the island for is—" But before he could accomplish the sentence the Earl had begun to speak, to explain—humbly, almost apologetically, yet with a humility not of obsequiousness but of reverence, his voice gentle, steady and quiet, his gestures restrained—as the voice and gestures of a man who hopes to convince by under- rather than over-statement are restrained.

"I suppose the nearest thing to it in myth or fiction is the island where Lotus grew," he said. "But it doesn't compare—it doesn't really compare. The Lotus-eaters knew indolence, not happiness. My island has happiness: it exists there as a physical and accomplished fact. I mean that in spite of what one is taught about happiness being an inward thing dependent on character and an outward thing dependent on circumstance, people are happy there. All the time. There is something in the air. Yes. I think that is it: there is something in the air."

Fitch, listening, was startled not into belief—he was as yet far from that—but into acceptance of an idea. It suddenly crossed his mind that people could be convinced. If they could be convinced of the justice of war in each successive generation or decade, for whatever cause or myth as long as it was comfortable to believe; if they could be convinced of the truth of iniquity, the beauty of a film actress, the value of aspirin and vaccine and aerial flight; if they could contemplate with steady equanimity the crucifixion of another race and the starvation of another creed;

if they could believe that beer was best or homogenised milk pure—then they could believe this too. It was simply a matter of advertising, of stating a lie often enough.

So before he even began to believe the kernel of truth in what the Earl was trying to explain, before realising with a shock—as he was to realise in a few moments—that he could command the support of physical fact and proof, he still could see the enormous commercial possibilities in the idea. 'Convince them they'll be happy in the place' he thought, 'and they'll believe they are. Why—there's no doubt. The one unprocurable thing sold like parcels of cake. Happiness by the pound.' The thought was brief, instantaneous almost, so that it merely filled a pause in the Earl's gentle narrative.

"No, it does not really compare," the old man said again; and this time his voice was a little troubled, as if he sensed the impossibility of his task of explanation.

The Minister cleared his throat. He was already beginning to wonder if the Earl's rambling and impossible tale would be concluded in time for him to get up to Whitehall by four. He refilled his glass and ran his thumb irritably round the rim. "The climate," he said, "really matters very little, I think."

But the old man was smiling a little, as a child will smile as it tells a story in its own way, in its own time. "Oh, I think the climate may be very largely responsible. Warmth, you know, and sun; and rain in its due season. But of course there is something else. I sometimes think of it as the Creator's storehouse of happiness. As if he had set aside this one spot where all things should be good. And when one comes to consider the magnitude of the universe such an act, such a setting aside, appears only as a very tiny miracle. Also, it is a gesture not without humour—not even without bitterness. To make the place small and unknown and to invest it with that quality of existent happiness as it is invested with air and light and beauty, so that by its mere size alone it may be restricted to nurturing on happiness the fortunate few—that, I think, is a gentle irony."

The Minister seized on a word. "Size," he said; "now that's one of the import—"

But again the Earl interrupted him, not from discourtesy but rather from necessity, as if he too was telling the story against time, grasping the clear points of its explanation while he could still believe in their power to convince, while the story was whole and vivid in his mind. "I must tell you a little of the origin of the place and people," he said.

It was then two-thirty. Fitch listened entranced until three forty-five. Long before the expiry of those seventy-five minutes he was convinced that the Earl was speaking the truth. Nothing could have been easier to believe than that the claim was merely a figment of an elderly imagination. One could easily have believed that the Earl himself was a genuinely happy man who in his happiness had developed the fixed conviction that the islanders, the retainers and subjects and peasants whose lineage was as long as his own and possibly in some cases even longer, were also of like happiness. Because a man with a home and land and everything in the world he needed maybe couldn't help viewing life and humanity through rose-coloured spectacles. But it wasn't like that. Fitch knew; he knew when a man was speaking the truth not simply as he saw it but as it was.

So he listened that afternoon to the tale of the island's history, its churches, its castle and its villages, its crops and its flowers and its people, seeing—or at any rate being aware of—the place as it actually was, so that its quality became for him an accomplished fact.

In the midst of the vast enworded vista of the island's history Fitch thought suddenly: 'The Minister's a dolt.'

The Earl's voice had been going on, level and gentle and unhurried and insistently courteous for upward of two hours now. He showed no sign of weariness. He had scarcely moved save to turn his head or raise his glass to his lips or—as if it gave him some kind of palpable sustenance—lift the rose to his face. The Minister, on the other hand, betrayed a kind of unctuous weariness. In the mirror Fitch watched the polished segments of his head turn away. From time to time he looked at his watch. His imagination boggled at the story the Earl was telling : he believed the old man to be in his dotage, a wearying old man with an obsession. From time to time he had attempted to interrupt, to seize on some key word and interject, " Ah, now the actual location—" but somehow his sentences never got finished : the subdued, level, mannered voice went on steadily, taking up the thread of narrative where perhaps half a minute before it had ceased as if to allow the burden of its message thus far to be comprehended, and the Minister was forced to listen once more— or possibly more likely to half-listen to this story that to him was both peurile and irrelevant and half let his mind play with sundry domestic details of his life.

But at last the Earl's voice ceased. " I am the last of the line," he said. " I have outlived my wife, even my children."

" I thought you said the island was a happy place," the Minister said with an almost belligerent tone.

" They died," the Earl said. " Where is the unhappiness in that?"

" Well, if you look at it that way." The Minister edged forward, his fingers drumming. It was three-fifty. " Now if you'll give me the plain concise details of the size of the island—"

" Tell me," the Earl said, " why are you so interested in the size?"

"I tried to explain to you at the outset," the Minister said umbrageously, "that we want the place for a target."

"Target?"

Impatiently the Minister whispered: "The bomb. Of course, the bomb."

Again the Earl lifted his lapel and smelled the rose. Again he smiled, this time as at some secret inner amusement. "You want to make an end to the place, obliterate it?" It was as if he in his turn now failed to grasp the import of the other's words.

"Difficult days; after all, these are difficult days." The Minister flicked impatient glints with his monocle. "One must do what one can."

"Yes." The old man turned away now from the other. Fitch could no longer see the features, the repose, the gentle incomprehension. The waiter hovered; at the far end of the room two men rose and moved toward the card room like lovers keeping an assignation. The afternoon was settling down. Faintly through the closed windows came the diminished sound of a bus back-firing. The Minister fidgeted, preparing to go. "Perhaps Drew got me here on a wild goose chase. I think we're at cross purposes."

"Perhaps. Yes, perhaps. I had envisaged some other use for the island. Well, no—I could not with truth say envisaged. I'd thought that someone with imagination, a statesman, even a business man—"

It was here that Fitch rose. In that room of dusty gloom even his departure was unobserved. Nonetheless he did nothing that might draw attention to himself. In the hall he told a page to get him a taxi. While the boy was getting the taxi he spoke to the commissionaire. "A discovery," he said with patent glee. "A yellow-label Ysaye. I want to get there before someone snaps it up."

27

" I'm sure I hope you're lucky, sir," the commissionaire said.

" Yes, yes," Fitch said dreamily; and gave the driver the Soho gramophone dealer's address. Of course it would put the commissionaire off the scent. Fitch enjoyed being subtle : it was one of life's minor pleasures.

At Shaftesbury Avenue he paid off the cab and took another. " The Mountalban Building." He leaned back on the ribbed leather. The glow of self-importance threaded warmly in his veins. He was like a child who has been given an errand to do and for the first time realises his potential value to the community. It was a familiar feeling. " Hurry," he called through the glass panel, the myopic eyes bright, the bismuthetic rumble in his stomach ignored now, as a soldier going into battle will ignore a twinge of toothache.

The Mountalban building was in a street behind Park Lane. Nothing about it had been altered, there was not even a sign on the Regency façade. The three houses that were classically surmounted by the graven pediment had simply been internally linked by communicating doors. Outside, they were creamwashed and dustless, and on either side of the main door was affixed a small bronze plate bearing the Mountalban symbol : MI. Nothing more. Mr. Mountalban had a horror of commercial vulgarity.

Fitch entered the building and went upstairs. Minor executives smiled weakly at him in carpeted corridors. Fitch was an outside man and they were desk-and-telephone men and there was a gulf between them. Resentment moved in Fitch like an ill-chosen meal; but he was aware of his own worth and took no offence. He was happy in the knowledge that he alone had immediate access to Mr. Mountalban, day or night.

" Mr. Mountalban," he told the third secretary. He

took off his glasses and polished them, aware of the need for some activity to control his excitement. "It's urgent, urgent."

There was a delay of perhaps half a minute; then at the end of it he stood in the room that might easily have been the reception room of a wealthy power's embassy save for the small walnut desk set to the right of the fireplace and the tape machine ticking with faint, even and inexorable motion its white ribbon onto the carpet.

Behind the desk Mountalban sat in the bright downglow of the bare, girder-like adjustable lamp. There were papers spread before him; they were few and simple, like the furnishings of the desk—letters of three and four brief paragraphs, a memo pad with a single row of figures, a thin packet of scrip encircled by an elastic band. The pen Mountalban held was the kind that can be bought at any village shop for three pennies—a thin brown stick with a J nib thrust into its end. He signed the last of the papers without haste, pausing on the 't' of his name. The stationery was good but not luxurious, the symbol MI was printed, not embossed, above the single line of type *Mountalban Investments* and beneath that was centred *London* and beneath that again a telephone number. Nothing else was necessary.

"Yes, Mr. Fitch?"

The words were neither invitation nor warning nor welcome; the voice was thin, suburban, and faintly—very faintly—obsequious, as though Mountalban had assumed not only the clerkly clothes (the bowler hat and the dark chesterfield overcoat and the rolled umbrella were put away in the closet, but there was no doubt of their existence) and the gestures and the faint ink-stains on the fingers but had taken on too the Streatham voice and the Streatham gentility and the dim but unmistakable servility of the 8.40 up.

It was not that he had never lost this suburban quality but rather that he had acquired it, perhaps believing that it could counterbalance some of the ventures that occasionally twisted in his mind like shame—Consolidated Milk Bars, Novelties Ltd., *The East Midland Gazette,* Neon Arcades. They were business successes, some of his earliest and best, but they rankled still. Nowadays he went in for property, airlines, chemicals, steel, armaments, building; there was a clean dignity about such things. But there were the others, the foundation stones, on balance sheets and agendas, reminding him that he still controlled pin-table saloons, printers of gaudily salacious literature, manufacturers of joke novelties and chain cafés where urns steamed behind misted windows and cigarettes serrated the edges of marble-topped tables with the brown stains of their burning. Such ventures had always been discussed in the places where Fitch's ears were listening; and now Fitch was here once more.

Mountalban sat upright. The round spectacles reflected the light and the room in miniature, the pleasant walls with the landscapes that for a while one didn't realise were originals, the silver humidor, the decanters and bottles on the Sheraton side table. His hair was greying at the temples and thinning on top, in the kneehole of the desk his feet in polished boots and undistinguished grey spats were visible tidily together. The effect was entirely clerkly; only the voice ran faintly untrue, for beneath the hint of servility ran an edge of coldness, a ruthless and petulant quality of threat.

" Something for me? Some news?"

" Yes." Fitch nodded. " Big. Oh, yes—you daren't, you can't, ignore it."

" That's for me to say." The cold edge was like a warning, but Fitch only laid a finger alongside his big sallow nose. They were like king and jester these two : outrage was privileged, rudeness condoned. " I'll sit down. It's a longish story."

The two men faced each other across the desk. Fitch touched the lamp and the downward cone of light vanished. " Too strong for my poor old eyes." Both men seemed to become part of the background, to be absorbed into the shadows : it was an ability they had both acquired for different reasons and now in the glowing dusk of the firelit room it seemed to unite them with singular umbilical purpose to some remote and common cause.

" It's about an island," Fitch said. Then he began without haste to tell the fabulous tale of the island where people were happy. It took perhaps the better part of an hour, Mountalban listening, from time to time interrupting, unwilling to believe yet believing, believing in Fitch's hunch as a man will believe in a woman's intuition and at the same time deride it, partly from superstition or fear of the consequences of unbelief, partly because Fitch had always been right before and therefore warranted belief, and partly because he regretted paying Fitch £2,000 a year to come and give him information he didn't take advantage of.

" You mean you're convinced the Earl was telling the truth?"

" Yes. But even if he wasn't—"

" But you're convinced he was? You're really convinced? You don't think there's any possibility of his being in his dot—"

" Oh, yes, I thought of that at first. At first I didn't see what else it could be; and from first to last the Minister couldn't see either. The dolt. But I know when a man's just stating facts—keeping them simple so that he can't even accuse himself of being on the side of exaggeration, and knowing that if he hasn't much chance of convincing others that way at least he'll be able to feel right about himself, won't be able to accuse himself of painting things in too glowing colours so that he wonders afterward if he's made not only the others believe but himself too."

" But I can't see any reason, any understandable cause for this place's—"

" No." Fitch removed his glasses and polished them, glad of the opportunity for a little literary thought. " There are more things in heaven and earth—" His breath misted on the thick lenses and his thin yellow fingers made their small rotary movement with the silk handkerchief. " You don't see a reason, and I don't see a reason—well, perhaps not altogether. But in my considered view the place is as he says it is. And as such it seems to have possibilities as a commercial proposition." He ceased. A coal moved in the fire and shadows leaped. " Nobody's ever sold happiness before. You invite people there, charge them so much and they go away happy."

Mountalban's lips were thinly smiling. He might have been indicting an office boy who had been pilfering from the petty cash account. " You have a very great faith in people's gullibility."

" They'll believe anything."

" They tend to believe the glamorous hyperbole rather than the truth."

Fitch gestured with his hand. " You can make this glamorous enough, God knows. True or untrue, you can make it glamorous."

At once the icy edge of doubt incised the other's speech again. " Then you're not absolutely certain?"

" As certain as it's humanly possible to be on another's evidence—yes. But don't you see: even if it were not factually true, even if it turned out to be just a place of remarkable beauty, climate, tranquillity—don't you see that with a big build-up such as the advertising people—"

"Of course I see that." The voice was mildly impatient now. Then suddenly it snapped viciously: "Why does he want to sell?"

Fitch shrugged. "How can I tell? People do odd things. Perhaps even happiness palls after a lifetime of it. Perhaps he just wanted to pass it on to someone else."

"No," Mountalban said. Suspicion lay on his mind like lead. "There's some other reason."

"He said he was the last of the line. There wasn't any other reason. The old chap was too innocent to think of one." Suddenly shame twisted in Fitch's mind too; money and commerce and a lifetime of noseying in the cause of big business ran sore like leprosy. 'I'm through,' he thought, knowing it wasn't true. 'This is the last deal. Whether he bothers with it or not I'm through.' His needs were simple—the small Bloomsbury flat, a little music, the eternal dosing of his stomach's rumble; but he would always return to the old haunts, the places where information might be garnered, the sedate lounges where the last gasp of a moribund provincial newspaper was mentioned, the airport where somebody was departing for a big continental deal in nylon, the party where a new flotation was first spoken of. There was pride and vanity in following his big-pored nose, in the certainty of his own intuition. "Yes, he was too innocent to think of one."

"There's the possibility that he wasn't."

Fitch made a move as if to depart. "I've given you the information. You must do as you like. No doubt he'll find someone else to sell the place to." With deliberate malice he added: "Perhaps Mr. Prospect."

It was that that did it. Prospect was a rival—*the* rival would perhaps have been more accurate. He had floated a £2 million company that built holiday camps on the

33

coast. "He'd make a good thing out of an island like that—something unique."

Mountalban too prepared now to move. "Sometimes you go too far, Mr. Fitch." But they both knew Fitch couldn't go too far. "On your way out you can ask them to make my plane ready. If you would be so kind, Mr. Fitch. And also tell them to make an appointment for me to see the Earl."

"Where?"

"Where and how will be for the staff to arrange. I pay them for that very purpose, Mr. Fitch—just as I pay you for another purpose."

"One, I trust, that I adequately fill."

"So far," Mountalban said, his voice pleasant, steady. "So far, Mr. Fitch."

Fitch prepared to go. The pain in his stomach was beginning to bother him. It always did after an interview with Mr. Mountalban. The tension, he supposed. But he remained the jester to the last. At the door he turned. "It could easily become a national success. Easily. Like Guinness, or football pools."

III

CREECH looked across the small walnut desk at Mr. Mountalban and said heartily, "You can leave it to us with every confidence, you know. Given a co-operative client Barclay Pratt can make a national success of anything."

"Yes," Mountalban said. He knew what Creech meant by a co-operative client: one who allocated a quarter of a million to advertising. It was the amount MI had voted for the build-up of Happyland. " What exactly did you want to see me personally for?"

" Well, I'll be honest with you." Creech waited earnestly for Mr. Mountalban to signify his approval, but no approval came. " I'm chief ideas man at B.P., and I've been given your account to work on. It's up to me."

" Well?"

" I thought you might be able to help me a little." The pink embarrassment was the embarrassment of the schoolboy seeking help for a trigonometry problem. " I don't think I've quite got this happiness business straight . . . I mean, *your* reaction when you went over . . . I'm going over myself, of course . . . but another opinion . . ."

Mountalban despised Creech a little : he'd been given a job he was afraid of and he dared not refuse it any more than he dare bungle it. " I suppose you've got a family?"

" Have I not? Two boys and a girl. Why—"

" Think what happiness would mean to them." Mountalban rose and went to the side table and poured sherry.

" Oh, they're happy enough—"

" Think again."

Creech's spine prickled coldly. " I forgot for the moment. This line of happiness as a commodity is going to revolutionise people's ideas a bit."

" You're the man who's going to revolutionise them, Mr. Creech. And to do that you've got to be revolutionised yourself first."

Creech tried to hold the sherry steady. It was bloody ironic, but he felt like the man in the night-starvation strip —lacked confidence. Well, you needed a hell of a lot to hold a quarter-million pound contract. But from somewhere he conjured up the certainty that all would be well. " I'm revolutionised. I'm sold—right, left and centre. You

35

bet! This is the biggest smash hit ever. But I must admit I wish you'd decided on calling the place Elysium. It's got the classics behind it, that word."

"And what percentage of the population would know what it meant? Happyland speaks for itself—to everyone. Simplicity. I loathe vulgarity, Mr. Creech."

He moved over to the tape machine. Above him the Turner watercolour glowed. Witwatersrand, Imperial Steel, Consolidated Milk Bars, United Mortgagee Trust, Neon Arcades. "I like simple, sincere things."

It was true: he groped for them, as a scientist will grope for relaxation in a detective story. He created his own spiritual standards. They constantly eluded him but he was unaware of it. He believed he could evade the magnitude of big business at any time he wished. "I'll tell you this in confidence, Mr. Creech: when Happyland is launched as a national success I'm going to retire, live there myself." The belief urged him on, it was like the bibliophile's secret search for the rare edition among the sixpenny junk.

He had gone over to the island in his private helicopter and had been immediately aware of the anachronism of the machine among the golden fields. 'Only a man of spiritual sensitivity would notice a thing like that,' he thought.

But he was hardened enough to flaunt disbelief. "It's a pleasant spot," he told the Earl's chaplain, who was to show him the island. "But you'll have to prove—"

"I?" the chaplain said. His name was Thomas Loomes. "The island will prove itself." There was no admonition in his tone. He stood facing Mountalban in the small field of flax where the helicopter had landed. He wore a bright blue shirt and dusty flannel trousers. Whatever he thought of Mountalban's glossy black among the bright flax he only smiled in welcome. " My house is just down the hill there. If you'd care to refresh yourself . . ."

Mountalban was suddenly reminded of books he'd read as a boy—Ballantyne and Verne and Stevenson, adventurers landing in strange places and miraculously finding their own tongue spoken, graceful phrases of welcome, offers of clothes and food and drink.

" I probably seem a little archaic in my speech," Loomes said. " I've been away from the mainland many, many years."

" You weren't born here, then?"

" No. Brutus Robinson and I are the only two men who came later. When the world became a little too much for us, you know. And now you're arranging for others to come too?"

Mountalban stepped through the flax, his brown leather portfolio swinging against the stalks. He wondered if he'd encountered a snag. " You think the people here will resent it?"

" Why should they? Resentment is no part of happiness."

Mountalban paused and took off his glasses. He'd been a little startled by the beauty of the landscape. " I suppose they're practically perfect, these islanders : never think evil thoughts, never commit evil deeds?"

Loomes said in his faded pulpit voice : " They are people like everyone else. The same emotions live in them. But things like greed and lust for power lie dormant because they're useless. The little money that exists here is circulated round and round again—given to the Earl in rents and received back in wages. Our economy is simple : we export grain and wine and dairy produce and flowers. We import a few clothes, a few cattle and sheep, a few farm implements. It balances out. It has worked for a thousand years

37

—more. No man has anything his neighbour might envy."

"You mean the place is happy because the people are happy?"

Again Loomes smiled. It might have been at Mountalban's puzzlement, his need to have everything explained, the suspicion that belonged to the world he'd come from; or it might have been simply that he wanted to smile. "No, I don't think that. It isn't explicable at all. I think you'll see what I mean before long."

Mountalban remembered how he had gone over the island. It was a perfect spot, the kind of place he'd seen pictured in coloured postcards and travel brochures. But of course it wasn't just that. Greece, Spain, Italy—they had equal beauties of landscape and climate. But they hadn't the spell that was on this place. It was magical all right. It was just as the Earl had said. You felt something. You could call it peace, tranquillity, beauty. Actually, he supposed, it was the simple life. Happiness. No one had ever offered the simple life before, the ungadgeted world of pure essentials. No one had ever had the nerve to suggest there was decadence in advancement, that you'd be happier away from radio, television, telephones and newspapers. A return to the land. It occurred to him that he might become known as the Apostle of the Simple Life. It was good business to do something no one had ever done before. Well, perhaps a few fanatics had—mysterious sects and religions; but of course they never put a price on the simplicity to which they advocated a return; and people never believed in anything that was free.

Dimly Mountalban perceived that he was on the right track. Already he felt a kind of relief: Novelties Ltd., Neon Arcades, Consolidated Milk Bars—they no longer bore the same secret shame. This would be atonement. He took off his glasses and said aloud to Loomes: "I love humanity."

Loomes nodded in acknowledgement but said nothing. They were walking through a village of stone houses. Thin clouds faded across the sky, a warm wind blew from the west. "This is Bluecopse. My own village is Sumer—across the valley there."

Mountalban saw all the villages on the island. There were only a dozen of them. "Accommodation will be somewhat limited. But of course there'll be many who come just for the day. What more can they want but the fields?"

"How will they come?"

"Aeroplane: it's the only way possible for day trippers. Boats for those who purchase a week's or a month's happiness."

They walked on. Presently they sat on a low stone wall. Mountalban spoke, his voice low, puzzled, perhaps a little frightened: "I can't account for it at all: but there *is* something: a spell. You can feel it when you breathe." As if recalling Mayfair, efficiency, the shareholders, he added: "It's a pity we've got to introduce it to the public in terms they'll understand." He took a memo pad from his waistcoat pocket, wrote a single word: "I shall call the place Happyland."

"Happyland," Loomes said. "You believe, then?"

Mountalban leaned back against the wall. He had removed the black jacket and the spats and his waistcoat was unbuttoned. He closed his eyes and opened them again as a girl in a long bright skirt went by carrying a basket filled with rolls of coloured ribbons. She waved. "Judith Prince," Loomes said. "The storekeeper's daughter." Mountalban watched the girl out of sight. He closed his eyes again. He looked contented, benign, happy; but when he answered Loomes it was efficiency that toned his voice:

"I have never, Mr. Loomes, begun any project in which I didn't believe. That is, belief in its ultimate success."

39

He said now to Creech: "I believe in this thing with all my heart."

"Me, too," Creech said brightly. He was a man who viewed every angle, left no stone unturned. He was a graduate (Psychology) of Brasenose and knew all about people, including himself. But Mountalban puzzled him. The old boy was hard-headed as any business man he'd ever known, yet he'd fallen base over apex for this dotty happiness theme. However, the idea was firm enough; and it was a change from soap powders and artificial protein food for cats and dogs. Happiness was æsthetics, idealism. He'd never tried selling anything but products, packets, bottles. He had a long fair moustache and as confidence warmed him once more the moustache took on its proper sheen and angle.

He went over to the island and spent a week there getting angles, viewpoints, dope. He noted the topography, the climate—everything. He took with him a photographer and an artist to make a pictorial record for the brochure. He filled a 300-page notebook with details of interviews— Loomes, a comic character named Brutus Robinson, a shape called Judith Prince, a few of the old peasants and agrricultural types. Then he returned and settled down to work in earnest on the scheme.

Because of the size and importance of the MI account he had been allotted Barclay Pratt's best copywriters and artists. He also had a team of ideas men.

There was no question of a build-up on a basis of anything but the truth. Belief in the products he was selling was one of the essentials of an ideas man. It could be conjured up by a process of enthusiastic thinking. He'd believed in Wyter, the Soapless Soap, and in Van Goff Shimmering Nylons, and in Speef, the Meaty Roll. The success of their campaigns had proved that. That was the kind of truth he believed in. He knew all about truth being beauty and beauty truth, but you had to face publicity as it was. It was the biggest little game in the world, but it was all a gorgeous hooey, a hyperbole shouted louder than the next man's, and when you got to the stage where you couldn't shout any louder, then you brought dignity into it and whispered, you brought taste into it and got your artists elected R.As. and you soft-pedalled everything and started all over again.

So there was no need for him to wonder if the island was a happy place. He'd sold himself on the idea that morning he'd felt his confidence draining a little because the idea was new and, at first look, screwy. Just screwy. But it was no longer screwy. Just as Van Goff nylons shimmered like a cornfield and Speef had the taste of real meat, so Happyland was bursting with happiness. He set to work to say so in terms the people could understand.

He gathered his team together for a conference. " This is the biggest thing we've ever done, lads. And it's got to be good. Within a year I want every man, woman and child in the country aware of Happyland—what it is, what it offers. We can really go to town on it. You've got the press to start with, but it's got to be bigger than that. Hoarding sites, skysigns, public participation—everything. I want to get it to the stage where every cartoonist makes gibes at it and every radio comic gags about it; where nobody can walk for a hundred yards without being reminded of it; where people think of going for a spell of happiness as naturally as they think of going to their local for a pint, as naturally as they take an aspirin for a headache. That's the target. And it gets top priority. I want every idea— even if it's only for a throwaway—noted and filed, every notion for a novelty analysed and costed." His eyes had a quality of innocent joy, like the eyes of a schoolboy at a model engineering exhibition. " Right. Now co-ordinate everything with me; and get cracking."

They crowded out—a dozen or so young men in sloppy-joes and checked shirts and moccasin shoes. They lived most of the time on gin and benzedrine and cute dames, but God! they were a wonderful team. None better in the business.

With ideas co-ordinated he showed a plan for the initial campaign to his chief. Harwood studied it and was pleased. " It's good stuff, Alex. Have you got it costed?"

Creech ran a finger along his moustache. " Everything. There's a file on costing there in the dossier."

" These cutout figures along the railway are a bit extravagant, aren't they?"

" Not really. Three hundred of them at roughly mile intervals cost no more than a week's press advertising. And they're static."

Harwood looked down at the artist's sketch of the wooden cutouts. " Mother, Father and four kids." I thought the Min. of Town Planning told us to soft-pedal large families."

" But the Min. of H. want us to boost anything that will whack up the pop."

" Okay," Harwood said. He closed the dossier. " I'll look at it in detail later. Meanwhile, there's another tricky job I want you to handle."

Creech crossed his legs, held an ankle with his thin grubby hand. " Yes?"

" It's Tom Prospect. He wants us to take on this new holiday camp he's building up by Spurn Head somewhere. Just a straight press campaign, nothing big. It clashes with Happyland, of course. The ideas are similar in a way. But we can't let the Prospect account go. Tom's bound to find out sooner or later we're handling Happyland as well. I want you to convince him we'll be giving him hundred-percent service, that we're making two distinct things out of the two schemes, that it's not like advertising one soap powder at the expense of another. Can do?"

"Surely. The best thing's to play the game and let him have the straight truth."

Harwood shrugged. Whatever happened he wouldn't be taking any of the responsibility. "Do it your way."

Well, it was all part of the biggest little game in the world. He went to see Tom Prospect. "You'll have to follow him up to Hull or some awful place," the secretary told him. He's gone prospecting on the new camp site."

It was a bit of land beyond Spurn Head, joined at low tide to the peninsula by a causeway. The place was being bulldozed and dredged and shored up to become a site for five thousand red and yellow bungalows. Creech, in borrowed gumboots and duffle coat, with his zippered document wallet and his manner jaunty and good-natured, went plunging through the wet sand.

"How are things, old boy? Smacking ahead at a quick clip?"

Prospect was the born vulgarian. He cultivated the natty, expensive opulence of the cinema because it was the kind people recognised and understood. He knew what he was doing. He'd raised the money to buy this place with a snap of the fingers, and he stood in the middle of it now, flanked by his two principal executive assistants, cradling in his arms a miniature daschund.

"Smacking ahead," he confirmed. "Ready by next summer. Those geologist wallahs are telling me I may have to abandon the place toot sweet—one of 'em is, anyway. They differ like dam' doctors. I'm taking the risk."

He and his two assistants were like a trio of wise monkeys. No distance ever appeared to divide them. With Prospect as their axis they turned with him, viewed with him, listened to him, thought for him, and praised him for the brilliance of the ideas they dreamed up for him. Their names were Walt Earley and Maurice Werner. Apart from their gumboots all three men were dressed with insouciant elegance, Earley and Werner just sufficiently imitative of Prospect to be flattering.

Prospect smoked an expensive brand of cigarette rolled in black paper with gold tips. He had dainty hands. He waved one now, a gesture sweeping and elaborate, toward the dredgers and the bulldozers and the contractors' huts. "We want to add a new word to the language, something creative, something with subtle undertones. Got any notions?"

"I've got the very word," Creech said. "But I'd better tell you first—"

"We're doing a creative job here," Prospect said. Werner nodded. Earley nodded. "We're building on God's simple soil a place where God's simple people can be happy. It makes you proud to think you're doing that."

"Damn' fine," Creech said. "A heap better than Mount—"

"What I want Morrie and Walt to consider and concentrate on is creative originality. We're all simple men at heart, we've come up the hard way and we know the significance of things. We've got to get our hearts in tune with the simple people and create for them. Never mind the cost. Don't let's have our minds clouded with figures and calculations—let's abandon any idea of profits. Let's just ... create." He stroked the daschund's ears. "Did you say you're taking on Mountalban?"

"Harwood's taken on this Happyland scheme, much against my advice I mean, what a publicity bloke wants is something tangible—"

"Happyland," Prospect said. He turned to Earley and Werner. "Now there's a duff handle. If B.P. couldn't think me up something classier than that . . . Happyland. Well, blimey! fancy B.P. taking on a corny idea like that. The whole thing'll flop flatter than a cold wet fish's belly. It's a wonder to me some who call themselves business men have got the eff— eff—"

"Effrontery," Werner whispered from the corner of his mouth.

"That's it: effrontery. To kid the good simple people with a thing like that. Not a thing to offer them except scenery. Now my kind of happiness is real. You can see it all round you." He gestured with his hand. "Where those bulldozers have been there'll be nothing but jollity. Jollity, jollity, jollity. Jollity all the time. Something tangible."

"Right enough," Creech said. "You mean you couldn't care less about us taking it on?"

"I couldn't care less," Prospect said. "You can't do a thing without faith; and any clot can see you got no more faith in it than a mermaid."

Creech smoothed his moustache with his middle finger. "You've certainly made things easy for me, Tom."

Earley interrupted him. "I've been thinking, Tom."

"Good for you, boy. Well?"

Earley ticked things off on his fingers. "We can give 'em amusements, we can give 'em fairy lighting, we can give 'em comfort in their bungies, we can give 'em Ritz-standard food, we can give 'em joy of living. But there's something else, Tom: there's something dear to the hearts of simple people." He paused, but he knew better than to pause long enough for Prospect to have to ask him what it was. "A wedding."

Prospect nodded. The gold fag-end looked like a protruding tooth.

"Let's build a church," Earley said.

"You see?" Prospect said to Creech. "Ideas."

"A little chapel," Earley said in a hushed voice, "with stained glass windows and lilies of the valley and everything. Where they can be married. I can see it in the brochure—"

"'Come and be married on Holiday Island and honeymoon in heaven,'" Werner quoted.

Prospect moved a way off. He stood facing east, then north, then west. When he returned he said: "The way I see it now the amusement park'll be over there to the south. Five acres of it. Variety Division can have their fling there as they've never had it before. But even then they'll get jealous of Building Div with a hundred acres to cover with bungies."

"I bet Natural Development Div'll have a super time turning the rest of the place into a romantic wilderness," Werner said.

Prospect said: "We'll even have a little chapel on a hill. The bulldozers can make the hill from the earth they dig out of the sewage disposal scheme." He said to Creech: "Got any notions for a name for the place? Holiday Island's duff."

"I've got the very word," Creech said. "I only wish all our clients had your vision. What about Elysium?"

"I wouldn't have the same publicity wallahs as Eric Mountalban for all the fairy lights in China—not in the usual run of things. But this is different. It's going to give me a chuckle to see him giving you a quarter of a million to do the impossible while I get results from a hundred thou. I'm going to get a good laugh from that." He rubbed his finger and thumb together. Werner produced a banknote. "What's that mean, that Elysium?"

"It's a sort of fabulous country where the Greek

heroes live. It means a condition of alpha-plus happiness."

" Greek : that's class. Elysium. You're going to see things happening to that name. It's going to be as big a national success as pools. Or beer." He gave Creech the note. " Here—have yourself a drink."

" Well, thanks," Creech said. " I'll drink to Elysium."

" You won't regret it. Speedboats from Cleethorpes every half-hour. I'll send you all the dope as soon as Admin. Div. have got to work on it."

" I'll see you," Creech said. He returned to London and went in his favourite brasserie and ordered two gin-and-tonics—one for Happyland, one for Elysium. He sat drinking them alternately, pleased with himself for having coped pretty successfully.

IV

HAROLD Bassett sat in the refreshment room on Paddington station eating a Happyland Mousse out of a cardboard carton. He scooped the pink cream out with a matchwood spoon on which was printed *Are you happy?* and glanced through the pages of *Transcendental: a Magazine for Tomorrow;* but actually he was thinking with derisive amusement of his parents' astonishment when they read his note, which he'd just posted in the pillarbox on Platform 1.

It was a note written in the proper melodramatic terms, suburban and frantic; for he'd acted according to the best black sheep principles.

I'm going away. I'll be all right. No need to worry.
I feel the need to spread my wings a bit, but don't

expect you to understand why. No ill feelings. I still think of you, Arthur and Basil, as always.

He took his pipe from his mouth and allowed himself a smile. Yes, he thought of them as always. He'd been intending to add that Spinoza and Schopenhauer and Freud and Ellis were a bit beyond their ken, and he'd imagined his father getting them from the library and puzzling. But in the end he'd decided against it. They'd have enough to think about. The old man would puzzle it out with the Buffaloes and his mother would talk about human nature to the neighbours; Arthur would think him a cad and Basil would be shocked to the very quick of his horrible suburban little soul. And not one of them would get anywhere near the truth : that because he thought for himself he'd achieved the courage to break away.

And take Doris with him. He was waiting for her now. This was the Cheesmans' night at the pictures and she'd been keeping an eye on Daphne—a sloppy great schoolgirl who hadn't a thought in her head but hockey and Stewart Granger. She'd leave a note, too—he'd told her exactly what to say—and the next day the two sets of parents would go through the motions of putting two and two together and getting an answer that wouldn't be nearer than a thousand years to the right one. They'd think of it as something clandestine, faintly dirty, and wonder that children coming from such good homes . . . What a theme for a Compton Burnett or a William Plomer !—someone to satirize the whole stultified soul of the thing.

Well, Connolly had said in *Horizon* that people ultimately got the literature they deserved—literature and life and everything else.

He looked at the clock and then at his own watch. She wouldn't be here for half an hour yet. Two men at the bar were drinking beer and telling puerile tales clouded with smut. He watched the surreptitious admiration of postcards held below the counter's level, heard the subdued laughter. Confront these men with some honest orgiastic sex and they'd be shocked to the core. What was it Freud said about pornography? . . . He couldn't quite remember, but it was certainly something important.

Surrounded by the clatter of cups and the hissing of weak tea from the steam-clouded urns he withdrew into himself. He wasn't revolted: he was simply contemptuous.

Over the chair by his side was draped his new trench-coat. On the floor stood a small brown suitcase containing essentials for the journey and a book or two. He wore a soft grey hat tilted back at the angle the salesman had shown him. Until recently he had never worn a hat at all, but suddenly the hatmakers had started a campaign to boost business. Their posters assured the hatless that if you wanted to get ahead you must get a hat. There was a subtle undertone of flattery in the beautifully-drawn gentleman who had got ahead. Eventually Harold Bassett had bought a hat because he realised he'd been bending to the influence of the sheep-like multitude of the hatless too long.

He lit his pipe and felt for his breast-pocket handkerchief, tucked it in a little; then he drew from the pocket of his trenchcoat a lavishly-coloured brochure.

It was bound in scarlet suède-surfaced paper and embossed in gold with the single word HAPPYLAND. The pages were of heavy deckle-edged paper and the typography and layout were worthy of literature.

Harold Bassett admired the taste displayed. You couldn't get away from it, the best art was in publicity nowadays. (There had been articles in *Transcendental* that had agreed with that very reflection.)

Turning the pages, he was somehow vaguely aware of Mr. Mountalban's regret at having to have Happyland

49

written up in terms the people would understand; but a Picasso was none the less a Picasso because it had to be explained to the dunderheads. He wouldn't shrink from admitting he'd been dubious himself at first. It was more than a year since he'd read that bit in the *Evening Standard*, the first time he'd ever seen the word Happyland; and he'd scorned it then. Nowadays of course it was familiar, it had sunk in, you accepted it, you actually had to book ahead if you wanted to get accommodation. So Mountalban's method of publicity had justified itself. It was naïve, of course, but it got over; and if you had the brains you could penetrate the æsthetics of the thing.

He began to read the brochure, adding his own æsthetics as he went along.

> You are reading one of the most amazing stories of all time. There has not been a story quite like it or with its power of impact on contemporary civilisation since the beginning of Christianity. And since that first Great Story there has been no event that offers such lasting benefit to humanity.
>
> It is true that we can offer our product to only a few at a time—in this it resembles the miraculous healing at Lourdes—but we dream of a day when all the people of Britain shall have been endowed with the unique benefit of the most priceless of mankind's possessions : Happiness.
>
> In time, even—our dreams have long vision !—there is a less-than-remote possibility that an entirely new race may arise—a race of truly happy people. For just as the horticulturists can implant a new strain of colour or perfume into future generations of roses, so can we, we believe, implant the genesis of happiness into the future generations of humanity.
>
> We who have made available the secret of the Isle of Happiness have pledged ourselves to this end; and because we want to serve, above all, the century of the

common man, the little man who bears the world's woes and the world's work on his shoulders, we have contrived by miracles that would be unworthy of publication but for the ends they serve, to keep the cost to you infinitesimal in proportion to the inestimable value received.

The charges are set out on the art broadsheet which is inset at the end of this brochure; but before you remove the broadsheet and find yourself intrigued by the brilliant witticisms of Sogg's drawings, we ask your attention to the few pages that follow this introduction —pages that outline the history and the marvels of Happiness as it has been discovered on an island close enough to our shores to avoid involving you in heavy travelling expenses.

We make no apology and seek no justification for our enterprise. Happiness is something we all seek. To erect the signpost to its source—a signpost that can be followed at almost negligible cost—needs no justification. And to prove, as we seek to prove in this brochure, that Happiness exists in tangible form and can be acquired by merely completing the application blank on Page 63, is the sole aim of our nation-wide publicity campaign.

Now, with the prospect of great Happiness opening its lush and tranquil vista before you, read on.

*　　*　　*　　*

From the dawn of time the pursuit of Happiness has been the concern of all mankind. But not till today has it been realised that self-sought and self-made Happiness is not the genuine state. In our fallible human way we have for countless decades been approaching the problem from entirely the wrong angle, ignoring even the pointer erected by Tennyson in his immortal poem *The Lotus Eaters* in which he describes a land peculiar for the languid properties of its atmosphere—properties

51

induced, so science has now proved, by various factors such as geographical location, soil erosion, vegetable and mineral presences, and so on.

A research team was engaged at fabulous cost by Mountalban Investments. The team consisted of the finest brains ever gathered together under the auspices of one organisation. They were men and women experienced in the colossally erudite researches of the scientification of apparently inexplicable phenomena. In plain words—and this brochure for plain people wishes to keep to plain words—their business was to solve riddles.

They began with the assumption that if a land such as Tennyson described

> *a land*
> *In which it seemed always afternoon*

possessed its atmosphere because of certain geological, marine and aerological factors, then other places on the earth's surface, subject to different combinations of the same factors, might well be productive of different atmospheres.

Extending their researches, they discovered that there indeed existed a place which from time immemorial had been associated only with sorrow, with weeping and wailing and gnashing of teeth. The identification of such a place would serve no purpose in this brochure. Suffice it to say that with the establishment of a milestone in their researches, our team pressed on.

"If sorrow," they reasoned, "why not Happiness?" And for many weary months, in the back rooms of life behind a world unaware of their mission, a world itself weary from the cares of civilisation, they sought and sought again the formula—the formula that would lead them to an actual geographical location where Happiness existed in tangible form, where all the factors inherent in the qualities of earth and air and water combined to produce an atmosphere in which only Happiness could exist.

At long last their patience was rewarded. They came to the Directors with a scrap of paper—characteristically torn from an article of great utility!—on which were inscribed mysterious figures of latitude and longitude. "Here," they said, "is the spot we believe to be *the* spot. It's a small island north of the Scillies." With typical British understatement they added: "We've investigated the place and it seems all right. But there's a snag."

The Directors were unanimous in their decision that money should prove no impediment in the removal of the snag. "What is it?" they asked the team.

"The island is owned by someone—a nobleman whose family the islanders have served for many centuries."

This was indeed an obstacle of the greatest magnitude, but it was decided to tackle it with characteristic vigour and aplomb.

The entire Board of Directors visited the island, admitting that their first purpose was to prove the team's claim—about which they were understandably dubious—, their second, if that claim was proved, to use all their power to purchase the island in the name of humanity.

Their visit, it may as well be stated right now, was successful beyond their wildest dreams.

Arriving in mid-afternoon they were struck immediately by the absolute beauty of the place. Beneath an azure sky that would delight a painter of the lushest landscapes they feasted their eyes on incomparable scenic beauties—on silvery rivulets gushing forth from mossy rocks, on trees that lifted their leafy arms to the glory of existence, on gardens and nooks of a verdure unknown elsewhere, on familiar flowers of an intensity and hue rare in lands where Happiness is a sensation of infrequent moments.

"Here," the team said, "is the place where the Hand of Creation has remained unimpaired through the

53

ages "—at least, that was what their learned phrases meant.

They set about exploring the island and questioning the islanders, for they were determined, even though they had been immediately convinced, that there must be no doubt, that the people of the island should themselves give testimony. This they did willingly, and a selection of their testimonials is given in the photographic supplement at the end of this brochure.

The nobleman was next interviewed, but of the details of the subsequent transaction and the magnitude of the figures involved there is no need to speak. It is sufficient to record that the owner—an elderly man himself endowed with the Happiness of his domain—agreed unhesitatingly to pass on the benefits he had enjoyed throughout his life.

" I had often considered such a course myself," he said, " but the organisation was beyond my capabilities. I feel absolutely certain that anyone visiting this lovely spot will take away with them not only memories of beauty, but a substantial bounty of the wealth of Happiness that undoubtedly exists here. I have had many visitors," he went on, " and without exception they have gone away and lived long and happy lives; I myself have lived happily; and the islanders have lived happily. It must be something in the air."

The team could have told him what it was—in a long formula; but he would have been none the wiser. The important thing is, that Happiness exists there— to be partaken of by anybody.

The owner was of course offered a permanent tenure of his beautiful house on the island; but this he refused. " I shall leave the island," he said. " Nothing can rob me of my happiness now; and I have a hankering to travel a little."

Thus the first chapter of our enterprise was concluded.

Of the organisation that has gone into the continuation of the story little need be said. The natural beauty of the island has of course been left unaltered, for the secret of Happiness is that the Simple Life shall be left unimpaired. No radio, television, telephones or newspapers will mar your stay; but a few specialist members of the team of researchers are permanently installed on the island to help you recognise the Happiness you may well have forgotten existed. For true Happiness is known to so few nowadays that it may easily go unrecognised without the aid of a competent guide.

We hope that by now you will want to visit Happyland. It is not only a holiday resort : it is a unique place, a place in which, mysterious as it may seem, you can actually feel Happiness seeping into your jaded system. It is an ideal place for the recapturing of marital bliss that has gone astray; it is equally ideal for the newly-wedded or the betrothed couple. (There is a delightful chapel with a resident priest who can arrange all nuptials.)

Success is unconditionally guaranteed. If you don't leave the place feeling perfectly happy your money will be refunded without question.

Think now of the jaded life you lead, of the cares that bow your shoulders, of the thought of bills, of illness, of tomorrow's weather, and a thousand other things. Wouldn't it be a wonderful thing if you could face those cares—as the Islanders whose testimonials you will find overleaf have faced them for centuries—with philosophical equanimity?

You can. After a visit to Happyland you can face life anew. There's something in the air that makes you happy; and with Happiness in your life you can face anything.

Think it over, talk it over; then fill in the application blank on p. 63 and post it (don't forget your remittance!) today. Accommodation is not unlimited : there are only a few villages, and advance booking is already heavy. But whatever you do, don't forget—

A
VISIT
TO
HAPPYLAND
IS MORE THAN
A
HOLIDAY
IT'S A
FOUNDATION OF HAPPINESS

*　　*　　*　　*

WHAT the Islanders Themselves say :—

The rugged countenance and majestic stance of Mark Bickmore betoken the Happiness that comes from the full life. " Ma ancesties came over with the conqueror. One of ma great granddaddies took up with the Earl of Hurstmonceaux and the fambly's served ever since. I'm pilot o' what was the Earl's private barge. I gets up happy and I sets down happy. I sees no cause for otherwise."

Judith Prince, one of the prettiest girls on the isle, daughter of the storekeeper in the village of Bluecopse. Asked if she'd always been happy she curved her arms above her ripe-corn hair and sparkled : " Of course ! I'm in love. I've always been in love—with the isle."

This is the Rev. Thomas Loomes, the resident priest, whose Chapel of Divinity, in the main village of Sumer, is an architectural gem in the late Norman style. Chuckling over his pipe the Minister said : " Sumer is old English for Summer; and it's always Summer in Sumer."

56

Janet Tiptree is the woodsman's wife, a fine simple woman who looked puzzled when she was told that many people in the outside world didn't know what Happiness was. "Don't they?" she asked cryptically.

Brutus Robinson, one of the few inhabitants whose residency was acquired late in life. Mr. Robinson is a great yarn-spinner and beguiles many with tales of his early life. "I came here to escape foolishness," he said; "and by jove! I have. The place has grown mellow with the Happiness of successive generations. It's haunted by Happiness. It's a magical place."

There you have an untouched selection of the actual things people have said and felt. They are the things that you too can feel. Decide tonight. Post the coupon *now*.

* * * *

A
Mountalban *M I* Investment
It's safe

* * * *

Harold Bassett wished dimly that he could have had a hand in the writing of the brochure. There were some lines of Byron's he'd have liked to quote; very apt.

> *There is a pleasure in the pathless woods*
> *There is a rapture on the lonely shore,*
> *There is society where none intrudes*
> *By the deep sea*

57

But of course you daren't go beyond Tennyson when you were dealing with the multitude.

The two men at the bar were preparing to go. Then one of them replaced his foot on the rail, said with mildly salacious joviality, " Wait a minute, Charl. I never told you the one about the honeymoon couple who come back from Happyland with—"

Then Harold Bassett saw Doris enter the refreshment room. She wore a blue mackintosh and carried a head-scarf loosely in her hand. The scarf was printed with a design of green clouds and purple kingfishers and the word Happyland repeated in different scripts.

He took his pipe from his mouth and rose to meet her. " All right?"

" Yes, I suppose so. I left the note. I don't want to think about it much." She smiled as if for a photographer who used palms and columned backcloths. " I hope it'll be all right."

" We're going away." With the stem of his pipe he marked each word. " We're going to live on Happyland for three weeks, then we're going to be married. Then we're coming back and we're going to start life properly. Isn't that simple enough to understand?"

She didn't like appearing stupid, and she knew he hated her to do so, " But I can't help sometimes thinking this island place might be the teeniest bit . . . sort of dull. I mean, there's nothing—"

" Not *teeniest*," he said spitefully. " You've been collecting slop-words from Daphne again." With immense concentration he said: " Happiness is not a dull thing. If only I could make you realise the aesthetic side of it." He tapped the brochure with his pipe. " The way they put it here's all right, but it leaves out all the idealism of the thing."

" I suppose it does."

She supposed it did. Honestly, he knew sometimes she hadn't a clue. Secretly, he knew, she'd have chosen a Prospect-Before-You-Camp—oceans of vulgarity, amusement parks and dancing on the lawn, organised romance, organised fornication. But his tolerance wouldn't stretch that far—not when their whole future depended on a foundation of happiness. " If you had a baby I bet you'd want to feed it on sugar-knobs instead of halibut-liver tablets," he said.

" Oh! Harold," she said.

Sighing, he said : " Try not to be arch."

Outside, the station echoed to the train announcer's bedside voice : " The train drawing into Platform 1 is the Happyland Express, leaving at midnight and calling at—"

" We'd best go," Doris said. " Hadn't we?"

Resisting an impulse to correct her ' best ' to ' better ' he said : " No need to fuss. Our seats are reserved."

" I'm sure I don't want to fuss," she said huffily.

He went to the counter and returned with two cups of tea. " I'd like a dry martini, but you couldn't trust them to mix one here."

While she was drinking the tea he opened the evening paper. With his pipe stem he tapped a half-page advertisement. The flat bonhomie of Tom Prospect grinned toothily up at them :

> *The kind of Happiness I offer at Elysium is the real honest-to-goodness kind. No bones about it. We spell it Jollity,* Jollity, JOLLITY. *It's tangible; it's there; it's REAL.*
>
> *Plan your nuptials for the chapel on the hill. Honeymoon in Elysium and live happy ever after.*

*Five acres of amusements. Romance in a wilderness
of love and moonlight. Life. Laughter.*
A few vacancies still left for the summer.

" I suppose really that's the sort of thing you believe
in?"

She said, " Well, that's only an advert, and anyway
Happyland does the same kind of thing."

He laughed rather pityingly. " Oh come! That jollity
stuff doesn't fool me for a minute." Then he flapped the
brochure in the air. " There's some difference between
that and this. Good taste and vulgarity. It's a matter of
chalk and cheese."

Uncertainly she said : " It's a matter of two adverts to
me."

Patiently he sought in his mind for some way of explaining. The puffs of smoke from his pipe broke and faded.
" Let's look at it this way : just because an idea's a bit
beyond your scope of comprehension you disbelieve. You
can understand amusement parks and sentimental slop
about chapels in the moonlight because they make an
appeal to known reactions in your mind. But when it comes
to something outside the scope of your experience you're
foxed. That's because the whole theory of Happyland's a
break with tradition. It was bound to meet with stone-
wall opposition from people like—well, people like you,
for instance. That's why the build-up's been in the broad-
est possible terms. They've had to drum it into people with
a hammer, but they knew they'd win in the end because
what they're saying is true."

" How do you know it's true?"

" Well, it gets round. People have been there, risked
it, found—"

" We don't know anyone who has."

He let his eyes roll upward. " God!" Then he resumed his patient exposition. " Years ago there was a man who stood on London Bridge with a tray of sovereigns, offering them for a penny each; and not a soul bought one. Why? Simply because no-one would believe in something that was against every tenet of human nature. We're up against much the same sort of thing here. It—"

She put her hand out and touched his sleeve. " Whatever does it matter anyway, Hal? We've decided and we're going there; and we're going to have a marvellous time."

Wearily assenting he said, " That's it." It wasn't the concurrence he'd fought for; but of course it took years to imbue people with aesthetic appreciation. Years and years.

V

THE first part of the concert ended with the Beethoven C sharp minor Quartet. There was appreciative but subdued applause but Fitch did not join in. He believed that music should be treated as something sacred, that one should not disturb the silence in which it hung suspended. If anyone challenged his opinion he always made an analogy of pictures and asked, " Would you scribble on the mount of a Blake watercolour or a Bewick woodcut? The picture's surrounded by a blank space which draws attention to its beauties. It ought to be the same with music. There ought to be silence for at least ten minutes both before and after a performance of something great." But applause had become a custom, people did it without thinking, many of them meant nothing beyond their expression of relief, others simply that they had detected no wrong notes in the playing.

The players went through the door that led to the artists' room. The cherubs and nudes gazed sightlessly down from the painted half-dome above the tiny stage. The long thin hall with its plush seats and green panels and tired gas jets began to empty. Fitch had no desire to move but he moved automatically toward the foyer where people would be talking, where things would be said. The habit was indestructible now.

In the foyer with its plush and gilt sofas the small audience grouped itself in pairs and trios. A few wandered off down the narrow vestibule with its rack of art paper leaflets advertising the forthcoming concerts. Beside the box-office a dowager with a deaf-aid stood fanning herself with her programme. She wore an ancient velvet evening dress and her face was thickly enamelled. She looked with condescension on the uniforms and hacking jackets and corduroys, the girls in sweaters and Burberrys and office dresses, even the few men in evening clothes—they were all part of a life that bewildered her : Fitch could see that.

He put on his spectacles and stood in a corner where no light fell, looking round. There was nothing worth hearing here. He permitted himself one of his literary thoughts : 'Truly a cross-section of society, united only by the love of music.'

Then the dowager was joined by her escort, an elderly man with bow legs and quilted velvet lapels to his faded dinner jacket. Fitch slid a little nearer, polishing his glasses. It would be nothing but small-talk, but listening to a particular kind of small-talk was his allotted task at the moment.

The old man bent nervously toward the microphone concealed beneath the dowager's wrap. " What do you think, Millie?"

" I think it's ridiculous, it's defeating your own object." She spoke in a deep angry whisper. " Take the Albert Hall and be done with it. A popular pianist, a popular pro-gramme—and there you are. Anything like this would be hopeless. You can see for yourself." Her voice ceased in a dying hiss and her eyes seemed to change colour. " If you must raise money to send people to Happyland, that's the way to do it."

" But quartet music's so beautiful," the old man said. There was a pathetic regret in his voice. " However, I suppose you're right."

" Of course I'm right. The only point about a charity concert is to raise money."

Fitch went back to his seat. He didn't want to miss the Debussy. When it was over he went slowly with the chatter-ing audience through the foyer and the narrow vestibule into Wigmore Street. There was a taxi or two, a few ancient limousines. He stood by the railings, shadowed, invisible. When he glanced back down the vestibule the electric lights had been extinguished, only the jets flickered on as the attendant came toward the door, keys in his hand.

Fitch faced toward Oxford Street. His appointment with Mr. Mountalban was for 9.30. There was time to walk off the wind in his stomach, perhaps collect another word or two.

Two girls who had paused to look in the *Times* book-shop window came sauntering on toward him. Fitch ex-perienced his rare feeling of incredible loneliness. The Beet-hoven had affected him like pain and the Debussy lay thin on its intensity like a veneer. The two girls turned the corner and Fitch caught a scrap of their conversation.

" . . . so I told Beales I wanted the middle two weeks in October. Because Myrna said she went there in the middle of January, she'd been staggered to that, and the weather was like spring, she said; and every day . . ."

" Every day. Happiness every day." Anonymous and respectable, Fitch walked down into Oxford Street. Lilac dusk on the pillared façade of Selfridges, the red, green and amber glints pricking the long perspective eastward. A newsvendor's placard flapped in a doorway: *Government seeking new bomb target?* Fitch took a paper from the bundle and dropped his penny with the others; but it was only a journalist's guesswork. The government might consider one of those tiny islands in the Outer Hebrides, the Special Correspondent believed. Fitch flicked impatiently through the pages. He seldom bought a newspaper. They depressed him.

One of those advertisements in the form of an intimate letter between two women quartered a page: . . . *and my dear, I have it on unimpeachable authority that the scrap of paper on which the Happyland formula was written was a sheet of Coronet Imperial, the toilet paper that is better than any* . . .

Fitch folded the paper and put it away in his pocket. At the Circus he turned south. He still had plenty of time. In Coventry Street a Neon Arcade and a travel agency stood side by side and a skysign spilt a scribble of words downward from the fading sky. *Are you happy?* In the pintable saloon there were two new machines: Happyland Quiz and Target for Happiness. Fitch moved on past the travel agency. There was dignity there, Bluecopse and Sumer and the landscape beauties had been painted in oils and framed in gilt, and from 9 a.m. till 5 p.m. the staff would be willing to answer any questions pertaining to Happyland.

Looking round, moving silently among the shifting crowds. Fitch felt a vague pride. Everywhere and everything echoed his enterprising conscientiousness—the Happyland clothes in Simpsons, the picnic baskets in Fortnums, the cocktails in Odenninos. He had implanted a new hope in mankind, a new game in its language. His thin chest swelled a little as he walked in their midst and smiled with the knowledge that no one knew him.

At the Mountalban Building Creech was alighting from a taxi. He held his zippered document wallet between his knees as he paid the driver. " Well, goodnight," he said with boyish enthusiasm. " Happy Landings."

" In Happyland," the driver said. He didn't smile. " I could do with a basin of that, I could. Elys*ee*um—that's where me and the gooseberry go, come next year. That's what I want: bring on the dancing girls. I couldn't never be happy in that other place—not with no dodg'ems, no dancing girls, nothing."

Creech leaned confidentially forward. " Forty-nine thousand other people thought that and found they were wrong. It's just a thought."

" You wouldn't have a interest in the place?" the driver said, slipping his clutch.

" Yes, and in the other one too," Creech called over his shoulder. " It's all the same to me."

He went on up the stairs humming the new Drury Lane waltz *Dream of Happiness*. Fitch padded up behind him, a flight behind. He wanted to belch before he got into the presence and the slow ascent would help.

Mountalban sat behind his desk like an elderly gnome. The thinning hair was ridged where the now closeted bowler hat fitted and he pressed the tips of his fingers together. " Mr. Fitch. Mr. Creech."

65

Darkness had come now, the blue velvet curtains were drawn, the room with its impeccable glass and silver and wood and tapestry glowed in the lamplight. Creech pulled at the knees of his trousers and leaned his wallet against the desk. " Splendid news, sir. Splendid."

Fitch sat doubled limply in his chair, his spectacles in one hand, a finger of the other laid alongside his nose. " Item, a couple of society people are getting up a concert in aid of holidays in Happyland for reduced gentlefolk; item, a party dimly connected with my landlord said she's drawing all her savings out to live there for three months; item, a comedian at the Palladium made another joke about the price of happiness; item, novelty notepaper, crêpe paper hats, watercolours framed in passepartout, ladies' garters and a Happyland pork pie have all been put on the market this week; item—"

" I'm aware of that, Mr. Fitch, since my own companies are sponsoring them."

" Damn' good idea," Creech said. " Of course when you're controlling—" He ceased as he saw Mountalban's expression. " Actually, I think I must lay claim to the success of our advertising. I know you think it's had its own vulgarity, but you must believe me when I assure you that there's absolutely nothing to be gained by being ivory-tower when you're introducing something to the multitude. You've got to knock it home in terms they understand. Other—"

" We've been through all this before, Mr. Creech. You know your business. I pay you to do what's right. If I object to it personally that can't be helped. But I want the tone raised a little from now on. Gradually."

" Raising the tone will not necessarily raise the sales, you know sir. In fact—"

" Mr. Creech, I have every reason to believe that in a

66

little while ' sales ' as you call them will be as much as we can cope with."

" But if you lose your publicity hold on the public, sir—"

" Mr. Creech, the most potent form of advertising that exists is the recommendation by word of mouth, between friends, between strangers standing in a queue, between two men standing in a bar. And that is what is happening now. People are discovering the truth behind the idea of Happyland." He touched a folder on his desk. " There are letters here from people. They have touched my heart."

Fitch held his hand to his mouth. " Manners," he said with dim suburban solicitude. " Tell people what to expect, lead them to believe they've acquired it and—hey presto ! They will have."

Drily Mountalban said : " A different sentiment from the one you expressed the day you came to me from Cradle's Club. ' And you're convinced the Earl was telling the truth?' I asked you and you replied ' Yes.' You replied in the affirmative, Mr. Fitch. You were certain then."

" So I was. So I am. I'm just putting the thing in Creech's light. Don't you see? Besides, I want to move on. Fresh fields and pastures new."

" There's nothing for you to move on to, Mr. Fitch. Nothing bigger I can tackle. You must spend your life now with your ear to the pulse of the humanity you have benefited. You might even have a little holiday, go to Happyland yourself—at staff rates."

" No," Fitch said. " I'm happy here, where I am. I can bring you information. You can use it or not as you please. I wouldn't be happy anywhere else." He looked pathetic-ally at Creech. " A dormant duodenal."

Ever his clients' best friend, Creech said : " We run a

pretty good campaign for Dr. Link's. Their stomach powders are supposed to be good."

" Just bismuth, peppermint, bicarbonate. Why should I help to pay your salary and Dr. Link's too?"

" He's been dead for years, old boy," Creech said jovially. " Donkey's years."

Mountalban said with cold impatience : " I am singularly uninterested in both Fitch's stomach and Dr. Link's demise."

When Creech and Fitch had given Mountalban the latest progress report and had gone—it was by then nearly midnight—he leaned forward across the desk with his head in his hands. He was alone and quiet and his spirit was in pain. He thought, ' It would be pleasant to go home. A day's toil and then home' But he was home already : on the floor above the bed would be turned back, the nuns-veiling nightshirt ready to receive his flesh, the electric kettle ready to boil for his cocoa, *The Sorrows of Satan* turned face downwards on the table—it was a good book, a wonderful book, when he had finished it he began it again, it was the only book he ever read. Everything was there waiting for him, but like a child he wanted something different : a journey home, a light shining from a front door, a little woman waiting. He wanted all the things the dark overcoat and the bowler hat and the umbrella represented, he longed for mediocrity as a clerk sometimes longs for riches.

He rose and went to the door. When he opened it he faced Fitch. Fitch stood there patiently as if he had been expecting a summons.

" I—"

" You need someone to talk to," Fitch said. He had the look of an incredibly faithful dog. " Of course you need someone to talk to. I knew."

Mountalban pressed the button on his secretary's door so that the secretary should know he had gone to bed. Fitch followed, three paces in the rear.

The bedroom was furnished in green because at some now forgotten time someone had told Mountalban that that was the colour most restful to the eyes. He turned the switch of the kettle. " Cocoa, Mr. Fitch?"

" Just a little of the hot water if I may." He fumbled for his container of tablets and when the water was hot stirred two of them into a cup with a pencil. " It's such a relief."

Mountalban said : " What did you come back for?"

Fitch peered myopically into the clouded water. " I wanted to give you advice : go to Happyland for a while."

Mountalban mixed the brown powder, a level teaspoon-ful. He liked it thin. " Physician heal thyself, eh? Is that your argument, Mr. Fitch?"

He went to the window and peered out into Mayfair. His face was composed, grave. He might have been a bank cashier peering to see if the footsteps he heard were those of his daughter (the apple of his eye) home from the Palais. When he spoke it was with the soothing tones of a hubby. " I can see a couple down there in the street, Mr. Fitch. They're walking slowly, their arms round each other. You see such couples in Mayfair sometimes. They stray from Catford to see the sights and can't find their way back."

" You care about them?"

" Of course I don't care about them. Not *them*. It's what they will say when they part that frightens me. You know what they'll say, Mr. Fitch?"

" I know what everybody says now when they part. When I was a boy it was ta-ta. Then bung-ho. Then cheerio. Now it's nothing but happy landings."

" ' In Happyland.' Don't forget that."

" That's what you wanted, you know: the name of Happyland on everyone's lips, in everyone's mind and in everyone's heart, from Penzance to Inverness."

" Of course. One has to be ruthless in business."

Fitch said with the air of presumption to which he believed himself entitled : " I think you've been a bit over-ruthless—with yourself. You thought you'd get hold of something clean and—er—pure. You thought it would make up for—well, other things. But you've had to vulgarise it to make people believe in it. You've had to treat it as a whopping big fib "—the schoolboy phrase was like an echo of a past Fitch had never possessed—" because that's the only way they'll consider it at all. Because people have got that far from truth : they wouldn't know it if they saw it. That's where your disillusionment comes in. O yes."

Mountalban had not turned from the window. " You like to think you're a perceptive creature, eh Mr. Fitch? That you know human nature?"

" I flatter myself."

" You do indeed." Now he came from the window, stirred the cup of cocoa, sipped it and set it down again. " And you may be right. Partly right." The voice was lower now, subdued, a little fearful. " I have been all over England—literally—in my little helicopter machine. The air route to Happyland is marked with balloons two thousand feet up in the air. They're anchored to the earth with cables like those barrage balloons we had during the war—in fact they *are* barrage balloons, government surplus; and long streamers fly out from the top of them so that when you look down you read ' Another five miles nearer Happyland.' Along the railway route are the effigies of the Happy Happyland Family—mother, father and the children. Everything is Happyland. It's no longer a stunt: it's a part of national life. And it frightens me. I look down and think of the people walking about below, the people I've drugged into belief."

" But it's true. You're offering them real—"

" Yes, its true. And frightens me the more because its true." He turned away from Fitch and began to sip the cocoa. " I have dealt so long in the lie and the half truth that I feel I've . . . contaminated—" Fitch heard the cup clink down. " I went over to that island and I was happy. I kept telling myself I was happy. But I no longer believe it. Or, rather, I believe it because I paid for my happiness and won't admit to myself that I believe it because I want other people to believe it—because it was the greatest commercial proposition that ever came my way. You see? I've hardened myself enough to talk about it, even. And now there are people over there every day, living the same lie. They've discovered that happiness exists in tangible form because I've told them so. So for them it is, as you said earlier, Mr. Fitch, just something they've acquired because they've been told it's there and they won't admit they'll believe anything—anything. They won't admit it even to themselves."

Fitch took off his glasses and polished them and took up the book. " I remember reading this to my grandmother when I was a schoolboy. The devil comes to earth disguised as a rich man." After a moment he said : " I see the government are looking for another target for their wonderful bomb."

" In a few days, Mr. Fitch, there will be another crisis —the existence of the bomb is being doubted. People are sceptical of the security offered by a weapon they are not even sure exists. And with the crisis bookings for Happyland will go up and up and up. People like to get away, you know. They like the best of both worlds—the ghastly and the beautiful."

Mountalban began now to undress. The black jacket and waistcoat were put carefully away in the wardrobe where two dozen other suits, all precisely the same shape and cut and made by a famous tailor, hung on hangers. The collar, the tie and the studs were put each in its ordered place; then the fine lawn shirt and the jaegar vest. He removed the trousers and pants after pulling the nunsveiling night-shirt on over his head, standing there like an elderly spinster in the locked bedroom of a continental hotel. "I sometimes see myself in the rôle of Satan, Mr. Fitch."

"Devils," Fitch said, "don't customarily dispense happiness."

"Again you're wrong, Mr. Fitch. They dispense anything. At a price."

Fitch slid silently away on his journey home to Blooms-bury. He was happy in the knowledge that Mountalban would never think of a breach of privilege. The jester was inviolate. He thought of the old queen and John Brown, of medieval kings who suffered their fools gladly. There was no affection between him and Mountalban : it was a relationship of simple necessity; they needed each other. But it was good to be sure of his standing. And sometimes, as tonight, he felt a vague compassion stir in him and felt that he should help. It was not solace he offered—solace and advice were always facetious, coming from Fitch—but an ear; 'an ear for the woes of the world.' Again he felt pride beneath his narrow chest.

He walked all the way, avoiding the places he should properly have lent an ear to. He was tired and he wanted to consider the music he had heard. Late Beethoven always eluded him—it was on a spiritual plane far beyond his comprehension; even the tonality would not fit into place; but the intense beauty that moved him like pain remained. There was no end to it.

He despised canned music, but like a drug addict he had to have some form of music available always. He had paid two hundred guineas for the elaborate handmade gramophone with its enormous wooden horn that rose from the corner of the room like a great air duct. He played it now in the dark room above the Bloomsbury green-grocer's shop—something to relieve him of the pain of the Beethoven. He chose the Mozart horn concerto, remembering the day he had found the set of discs in his usual shop —the prim assistant whom the proprietor always addressed as ' Mr. Bassett ' and whose secret passion Fitch identified as Tschaikowski and Liszt, though he'd admit to nothing less modern than Stravinsky. In the midst of the horn concerto Fitch wondered, for no reason at all, what the prim Mr. Bassett was doing at that moment. Vaguely a face clouded up, a girl's face, moving upward across an everlasting line of panelled advertisements—brassières and toothpaste and whisky and Hovis—beside the thin aesthetic cheeks of the Stravinsky enthusiast. He must have passed them on an escalator at some time. The girl, of course, was his girl. They were probably together now in some secluded spot on Streatham Common, imagining nightingales, surf, perfect peace.

Fitch's peace, Fitch's happiness, were in the horn concerto. He let it envelop him, completely.

VI

As soon as they had landed on the island Harold Bassett
had been ready with quotations. He had read them up,
secretly, like a student preparing for examination. They
were to bolster up his own belief as well as Doris's; for,
having paid his money, he was of course as ready as anyone else to be happy. He'd found Byron and Yeats and W.
J. Turner, and a lot of Shakespeare—they'd all written
about islands, rapture on lonely shores, happiness in golden
lands, wandering ever with woven hands, how far away
were the unquiet lands, *et cetera*. He had them all ready
to mind. He thought of this as coöperation, having the right
atmosphere ready in your heart. He planned to say as
they stepped ashore,

> *To an isle in the water*
> *With her would I fly*

and to follow that up almost immediately with

> *There is a society where none intrudes*
> *By the deep sea.*

He saw the two of them standing there and breathing
deeply and knowing, because they were receptive, that
happiness had found them immediately.

But in fact he had said nothing. He realised in time that
it would have appeared chi-chi. They had arrived at noon
and he had shepherded Doris forward across the quay, his
hand at her elbow and his pipe gripped tightly between

74

his teeth in the serious but considerate manner that would be suitable for dealing with any formalities.

There were no formalities. There was a guide—one of the specialist members of the team of researchers—and it was he who spoke first.

" Rest awhile. People sometimes bring too much haste with them, and it's all so unnecessary here, The sand's very warm." He smiled pleasantly and walked off toward a rock, where he sat down.

" That's that," somebody said.

For some reason Harold Bassett had imagined himself and Doris arriving alone. When they embarked with a batch of five hundred other people at Penzance he was momentarily surprised, though he wouldn't have admitted it; and in any case he made himself smile at himself, made himself think, ' Crackers. I must have been crackers, thinking we'd be the only passengers.'

And there they all were, disembarked and spreading over the sands for all the world like trippers to Brighton, bright tan suitcases and straw baskets and workaday clothes looking like the impedimenta of an alien race—as indeed they were, he reflected a moment later. It made him feel mildly embarrassed to think he had been ready with bits of poetry. He could see that it would have been very embarrassing indeed to say them aloud.

They sat down on the sands. Doris now wore a cotton dress and sandals. Harold had packed his trench coat and her blue waterproof away in the suitcase. He himself wore tan gaberdine slacks, a tweed jacket patterned with window-pane checks, and a cerise linen shirt. There was a leather watchguard fixed in his lapel buttonhole and on the other end of it, snugly tucked away in the folds of his breast-pocket handkerchief, was a joke novelty—a tiny naked black doll that squirted a stream of water from its navel into the beholder's eye. Harold Bassett abhorred such things, but he had bought it because he believed it was good to go against one's instincts now and again.

Doris turned suddenly and looked inland. There was an exotic beauty about the rising stretch of land : cottages clustered, shadowed by tulip and magnolia trees, there were coloured boats, an upward sweep of flowered acres, a crest with elms. Faint clouds fled seaward in the warm west wind and a lark ascending trembled in splendid song. Everyone in sight was silent. It wasn't only the beauty; it was the knowledge that happiness fell from the air at this spot, that here the Hand of Creation had remained unimpaired throughout the ages, that since the first Great Story there had been no story like this one.

To confirm their knowledge one or two now opened their brochures, murmured in Public Library whispers that the simple life had been left unimpaired all right. A woman in patterned dungarees (" Be happy in Happyland casuals ") sat a little way off from Harold and Doris. She clasped her hands round her knees. " My God," she kept saying. " My God. You *can* feel the happiness seeping into you. You *can*. You *can*."

Doris said, " I sort of expected they'd have . . . Oh, I don't know, a big sign or something, telling you this is it."

" Plenty of signs all the way down. Those sordid cut-out wooden figures ! It's wonderful just to see nothing but . . . perfection."

" Hal," Doris said. Ecstatic tears misted her eyes. " It is wonderful here. Oh it is !"

He jerked his pipe stem toward the dungaree'd woman. " She keeps saying so." But there was no malice in his tone. Unguarded innocence sprang in him, as it sprang in them all.

No-one made any attempt to move. It was as if time

76

needed no regard. In the secret places of the heart they had imagined a place where time stood still and had conditioned themselves to believe in it and it was so. They were in Happyland. They had paid their money and they were happy.

Presently the guide returned and walked amongst them. He held typewritten lists in his hand and began checking off names. " Rather like a school treat, eh?" he said. " There'll be wagons here for the baggage in next to no time. We've a few set aside for transporting those going to the more distant villages. I'll collect your accommodation cards while I'm here. It's a bit regimental, but it's the only bit of bureaucratic organisation you'll see here. And it really is necessary with an increasing number of visitors everyday."

" How many here?" somebody wanted to know.

" Now, with you folks? Capacity. Of course people are wanting to stay on after their term expires. They can stay of course; but they have to give up their accommodation for newcomers. A whole batch—a hundred or so —have given up their rooms in the villages for some of you folks only this morning."

He had come to Harold and Doris. " But where will they go?" she asked.

The guide lifted tanned fingers holding a batch of accommodation cards. " The sky makes as good a roof as any," he said; " and the ground among the stooks of wheat is soft and welcoming. You've forgotten the peace of the earth. Everyone does. But when you've been here a couple of hours more it'll all come back."

Doris said gently: " Yes."

Wagons came. They were painted in bright colours and the horses stood patiently while they were loaded with the baggage. Everyone helped. Laden with their prosaic suitcases and portmanteaux the wagons had a look of stealthy humour, as if they were aware that they should be laden with bundles and boxes and pots and pans rather than these decently-concealing boxes from another world. They moved off along the road that crossed the sand and twisted inland. The road and the whole landscape shimmered in the heat and Harold Bassett recalled a line from a poem he had once almost written : ' August's afternoon shimmers sword-like above the bee-buzz and the sward.' Often he had flushed, recalling it, recognising it for a feeble attempt; but now it seemed forgivable, even attractive in a jejune manner. He lit his pipe and the blue smoke thinned and vanished. " Well, we're here," he said with a gruff sentiment he couldn't control.

Another brightly coloured wagon came. It was a hay wain and it had been fitted with wooden seats along each side, sixteen people sat in two rows looking at each other with neither embarrassment nor hate. They were all thinking how remarkable it was, remembering with discomfort the way they sat in trains and buses. Harold Bassett thought, with a flicker of perception he gave himself no credit for, because he didn't realise it existed : ' We don't forget, then. We remember how we were before we came here. Useful. Like a yardstick.'

" I thought perhaps everything'd vanish, sort of," Doris said. " Memory and that; so it'd seem you were trying to remember a dream." She looked at him, anxious for him to grasp her meaning, which he did. " I thought it might be like that too," he said. " But it isn't, is it?"

" No."

" Goodbye now," the guide said, dropping the bolt in the staple that secured the flap.

" Happy lan— " someone said automatically; and suddenly they all saw the funny side and laughed.

" It happens every time," the guide called after them.

After they left the sands and began to climb the road they saw people in the fields, among the sheaved corn, some of them working, some grouped together talking, some eating picnic meals. They waved and those in the wagon waved back.

" Of course it was silly to think anything like that'd happen," Doris said. " It'd be sort of magic, like you read in books when you were a kid."

" Yes," Harold said with some stoicism.

The wagon took them right across the island. Bluecopse was their village. It was on the western side, a place with walled gardens starred with mesembryanthemum and with a brook running the length of the main street. The slopes embracing the village were of flowers and pasture. There was a vineyard bordering a stretch of river, and above it, cresting the highest slope, a great stretch of gentians into which a copse of poplars had been stuck like feathers. In the light of morning, and again at sunset, the bright blue of the gentians struck upward like a haze and tinted the trees. The effect was beautiful.

Harold Bassett had a room at the inn *The Lute Player* and Doris Cheesman was a few doors away in a room next to the village store. Both rooms were at the back-overlooking an orchard, and the walls were mapped with apricot trees in a thick network of veins like a river-map drawn in charcoal on the faded pinkwashed stone.

The innkeeper was named de Montfort—a ruddy, square-faced man in a wasp-striped waistcoat. He spoke in a grave-deep voice. " You're welcome, Harold Bassett. A room on your own at the back. One other guest only, and him permanent: Brutus Robinson."

" I know the name. Of course he's featured in—"

" Yes. Well, you'll see for yourself. He tells a good story—a thousand good stories."

" True ones?"

" Some true, some less true. Of course it doesn't matter. A story is a story."

Harold Bassett went to the open window. De Montfort stood behind him, stood there with a grave decorum that was neither servile nor impatient but was, rather, in some secret way, immensely friendly.

" My young lady's down the street."

" At Janet Tiptree's. Yes. If you lean from your windows together you'll see each other. You're going to be married, Thomas Loomes tells me."

" In three weeks."

" Well," de Montfort said. He stood with his thumbs in his striped pockets, nodding his ruddy face. " That's a good thing for all concerned. Especially you and Doris Cheesman. Warm your thin blood up, the two of you. Is she a bedworthy girl?"

" I—" He took the pipe from his mouth, felt himself flushing. He was enormously shocked; but he feigned unconcern. It was quite plain that de Montfort meant nothing beyond the plain question. There was no innuendo in his tone, no sly lechery in his eye. " She's very beautiful," he said suddenly, affectedly.

" Well, joy on your union. You must acquire the art of teasing her adequately first."

" Yes" he said with what he intended to be a smile of gratitude. " I'll remember that."

Harold heard de Montfort clatter down the stairs and return to the parlour of the inn. Leaning from the window he counted the houses to the fourth. There too a window was open and for a moment he thought he heard Doris's voice.

Doris was in fact speaking just then. "It's lovely," she said; "but somehow I thought I'd find you . . . the people . . . I don't know—different."

"How different?" Janet Tiptree said. She had coiled dark chestnut hair and green eyes, and was a fine-looking woman, straight and regal, like the queen of a diminishing nation who has joined unrecognised in a peasant dance to please herself. "That strange man Alexander Creech said the same thing. How different should we be? Like gnomes or sprites or something?" She touched her belly with complete innocence. "We're born the same way, from here, head downwards. There's no difference at all."

"Oh!" Doris said; and "Oh," this time more flatly, through lips dry with embarrassment, though she honestly thought of herself as a broad-minded girl, not prudish at all. Then, to relieve her own awkwardness she said: "But you're happy."

"So we are. And over there where you come from there isn't much happiness, Alexander Creech told me."

"No. That's why we come." She said archly: "I'm going to be married here."

"Well, a blessing on your bed. If you want a child from the first union you must judge very carefully the distance between the months. I tell you, not to interfere, but because my own daughter is without attention to this matter, and to be without a grandchild—"

"Thank you I'm sure," Doris said frigidly, "but both Mr. Bassett and I know all about that sort of thing. Actually we're very keen, and in England all that information's ever so easy to get at clinics. And Mr. Bassett read a Penguin on biology and genetics only the other day."

Janet Tiptree nodded slowly. "Well, that's a good thing. You'll hear plums falling in the night. The ripe ones.

81

It's a beautiful sound. Sometimes Robert Tiptree hears it too; then he holds me and touches me—O gently!— here, and it seems as if the sound and the fruit and his hand on my breast are all . . . one thing." She ceased and her hands moved. " You know?"

Flushing, Doris said, " Why, we're not even married yet." The words sounded thin and empty, as if they held neither truth nor meaning.

That night as Harold Bassett and Doris Cheesman lay in their four-walls-apart rooms they smelt summer and beauty and happiness. They breathed the scent of it. Beyond the open windows fireflies drifted and sang, and beyond, farther, the leaves touched in the orchard. All the day's dying was nothing but beauty and under the etched green stars nightingales held the distant copse and ravished its stillness with their calling. Faintly in the orchard darkness, as Harold Bassett slid into sleep, a ripe plum fell to the ground with a small thud and lay, bruised, adding to the smell of summer; and faintly on the edge of hearing, as Doris Cheesman deliberately relaxed as *Woman's Own* told her—toe, heel, calf, knee, finger, wrist, elbow, one by one—a plum fell with a gentle sound to the grass and she recalled for an instant an innocence she had long forgotten.

In the morning they met at breakfast. That was the arrangement : de Montfort was to feed them both. He didn't wait on them : the food was there on the table and they all sat down together. It seemed right that way.

" Brutus Robinson will bring his own fish and cook them. He likes them with no more than five minutes between river and frying pan."

Presently they heard him come in. They had not seen him yet, but his voice was enormous. While he was frying the fish he sang *Erlkönig*, *Frühlingsfahrt*, and *Widmung*, the songs booming round the kitchen, punctuated by the sound of hissing fat and salivary lip noises.

"He must be a big man," Harold Bassett said; "like Chaliapin."

"No," de Montfort said. "Quite small. Only the voice is big; and the imagination."

He came in then, three fish speared on the end of a toasting fork and a willow-pattern plate in his other hand; and he was indeed quite medium size, with a high bald head and dark eyes that hid quick thoughts. When he spoke it was in quite a medium voice too, pleasant but soft.

"Yes, well you don't have to tell me: you're wondering about the voice you heard. Mine—and you can believe it or not, as you please, for I don't intend to shake the rafters in here for the sake of being believed." He put the plate of fish on the table and hung the fork up on its hook by the hearth. "But once, years ago, when Caruso was blackened in the throat from smoking those cigarettes of his, I deputised for him and not a soul ever knew the difference. I was a stage hand, just a carpenter, but not a soul knew the difference." He sat down and began to eat ravenously. After a moment, with the forkful of fish poised over the plate he said: "There's more people than ever on the island. You can't move for them." There was no annoyance in his tone.

Doris looked toward the window. The village street was deserted; beyond it the flower fields sloped away. There were a few workers in the fields.

"Oh, you won't see them from here; but when you go out, in the deep places where there never used to be anybody but you and whoever you believed in—that's where you'll find them. Even in the streets of the villages, later on. I notice the difference, I can tell you."

83

" Harold Bassett and Doris Cheesman are these lovers' names," de Montfort said.

" Welcome too. Of course you know me by that red book."

Probing, Harold said: " You did say it—what it says you said? About coming here to escape?"

" Oddly enough, it's what I said, more or less word for word. But somehow the tone's got altered. I don't know how. Some alchemy I've forgotten about, likely."

Sunlight lit up the room, the brick hearth and floor, the lute on its hook on the wall, the flowers in their earthen-ware jars. " There was rain in the night," Brutus Robinson said. " A healthy shower. Shall you two be wanting direction anywhere?"

Harold looked at Doris. Their faces had that look of studied beatitude, like the faces of models posing as cherubs to a painter of the Holman Hunt school. " Well, we hadn't really decided. Thought we'd just drift, look things over—" Harold tried to force some kind of reserve into his voice; but it would not come, because he was happy.

The two of them started out toward the copse. They didn't speak because there seemed nothing to say. They were both aware of an immense and almost hurtful happiness. Whatever troubled them in normal life had not vanished but it lay now deep within serenity and didn't matter at all.

As they ascended the slope to the copse and stood truncated about the calves by the pools of gentians they saw that Robinson had been right: there were a lot of people. When they looked eastward across the slopes they knew more people were there than rightly belonged in the land. It was not that they were massed in any way, or even moving with any effect of numbers, as the crowds seethe

84

at Blackpool or Southend, but, rather, as though their presence suggested itself as the companionship of unseen friends will make itself known in darkness or fog. They passed a number of people, some whom they had travelled with the day before, and all of whom they felt themselves to be one with, in that same unmistakable manner of impeccable friendship that Harold Bassett had felt as he stood by the window with de Montfort.

They sat down at the edge of the copse to rest. Doris sat with her hands clasped round her knees and Harold lay full length on his back. There was something about them that was new, as if their hearts beat in choreographic unison with the young and unravished hearts of the islanders; but they were not unaware of it. It was as if the thin patina of self-consciousness veneered them even here.

" It'd be lovely if we were married now."

" Three weeks from today we shall be," he said. " No need to worry about that."

She trembled, recalling the night and the orchard and ripe fruit falling. " That Janet Tiptree almost—well, made suggestions . . . about us."

" The old innkeeper chap too." After a moment he said with considered insouciance, " We *could,* of course."

" O, no, Hal. I'd want it to be perfect. You know— unblemished."

He nodded, understanding. " I absolutely agree. The only thing we've got to remember is that it's by our own id that we act as we do. Otherwise . . . otherwise we'd just be a couple of conventional vulgarians." He clung, even in the midst of happiness, to his interpretation of life. " Otherwise we'd be Freudulent," he added with a straight face. But Doris, who had heard him make the joke many times before, laughed with exactly the right degree of enthusiasm.

"We really lift ourselves out of the rut by resisting temptations other people'd fall for," she said.

"Of course," he said, thinking obliquely of disgrace, of neighbours' whispering mouths, ostracism at the Buffaloes, humiliation—but turning the blind eye of a deliberate and essential cynicism, a derision almost true in its depth. It was the blind eye of the vulgarian who acquires taste, most of it bad, and is himself more easily hoodwinked into a spurious culture than the vulgarians he derides are hoodwinked into phoney joy, Hollywood bastard parlance, glamour.

He was thinking now of the psychology quizzes in the magazines. He smiled tolerantly when Doris did them— "They're only based on the vaguest sort of psychology, you know"—but he did them himself while sitting on the W.C. or glanced at them in public with the air of one engaged in Mass Observation. He'd convinced himself they were for amusement only, but he had a sneaking regard for their decision that he was something of a complex type, and sometimes he observed this agreeable complexity with satisfaction. It wasn't really important that deep down inside you were full of the worst kind of snobbery. It was the result of environment and you couldn't possibly help it. What mattered was that you were aware of it when you chose to be.

Below them a man crossed a stile and came on up toward them, skirting the gentians by the path. He waved while still at a distance and the air and the light were so clear that they could see that his thin curling hair was as yellow and fine as a child's. His faded blue shirt had odd buttons and his trousers bagged over worn canvas shoes laced with coloured bast.

"I'm Thomas Loomes," he told them. "The parson." When he touched their hands they felt the texture of his flesh, like brown sailcloth.

86

"You're going to marry us." With a certain coyness Doris put her hand in Harold's hand, remembering how he hated any public demonstration of affection and noting that he didn't mind now. It was as if all his principles meant nothing to him any longer because he wanted to show how happy he was.

Loomes looked down at them. "To live for the moment, each separate moment like a world of its own. There are many moments in three weeks. Maybe you won't want to get married by that time."

"Oh, we shall want that all right," Doris said, continuing the coy touch.

Loomes went. They watched him cross the downward slope till he came to a field where people were picking flowers and packing them in long flat baskets. There he joined with the workers in their task. Doris had a sudden thought: 'When he's finished down there he'll smell all over of flowers.'

Presently they heard in the distance Robinson's voice. He had muddled his songs a little this time, but Harold, with professional perception, identified bits of *Litanei, An die Musik* and *Frühlingstraum*. Liking things just so he called: "You're getting a bit confused, Mr. Robinson. It's—"

Robinson came through the trees and squatted on his heels beside them. "It's of no consequence at all. As long as the songs are sung." His quick eyes watched them. "I must tell you about a most remarkable thing—something really worth telling."

His face, they noticed now, was quite conspicuously ugly, deep-lined and loose-skinned, like the face of an elderly monkey. But the beauty of his voice was remarkable, so that as they listened they didn't bother at all about appearances, but only about what he was saying.

" Well, I was swimming in the river the day I'm telling you about and suddenly I opened my mouth to sneeze—just one of those sneezes that tickles you when you look at the sun. All right. I sneezed and I shut my mouth again. But what had happened? Why, I'd swallowed a drop of water. Nothing wrong with that of course; but it wasn't until afterwards that I remembered thinking, and not bothering much with the thought, ' I believe there was something in that drop of water '—something else than oxygen and hydrogen that is.

" So it proved too. A couple of days later I felt something dancing about in my stomach—here, just below the navel—and I wondered what it could be, it not being my habit to eat fish alive. I didn't worry, it not being in any way painful or incommoding. In fact I thought to myself that I was having a new experience and I told Thomas Loomes, ' I shouldn't be surprised if I'm having a child, and if I am I'm going to give the women a lot of scorn from now on, because the feeling's no more than a fidget.'

" However, in a day or two it began to get fidgetier, and I began to lose weight—for all I ate a dozen fish for breakfast on the third day, and had eggs galore, and more vegetables than'd go in a sack.

" And all the time the fidget was growing inside me. Twiddling and turning about, it was, like one of those automatic grenadiers they have outside Buckingham Palace —or did, in the days when I knew London. It's to be hoped they've got more sense now."

" No," Harold said. " They're still there."

Robinson sat down with his back against a tree. " The fools," he said with sudden immense compassion. " O, the poor stupid fools." Then, with a thought for his yarn; " But I was telling you about this strange movement inside me, this little creature."

" It *was* a creature, then?" Doris said.

" Of course: a tadpole. I'd swallowed a tadpole in that drop of water; and there it was inside me, stuck somehow, and turning into a frog as fast as it could—a fat one too, it felt like; and on my breakfast. Not that I grudged the creature anything, but it seemed to want all I put down. There didn't seem to be any way of diverting any of it to my own use.

" I went to old Mark Bickmore about it. He's the oldest man here and he knows a thing or two, I can tell you. He listened at my mouth. ' It's a frog,' he said. " I can hear it croaking.' I shut my mouth and said, ' Well, what's to be done?' He thought a minute and he said, ' Starve him out. That's the only way. He's snug enough down there, feeding enough to burst.' This didn't please me at all well. I was already starving on account of a frog. But it was the only way, it seemed.

" Well, I ate nothing at all for two days, and as I was already famished when I started it didn't make a lot of difference to me. But it did to the frog. I could feel him turning over and over, looking in all the corners for something he might have left; but of course he'd relied on me being ninny enough to feed him till allelujah kingdom come, so he'd not saved a scrap.

" ' Now's the time to prepare,' Mark told me. Then he went off down to the river and hooked a bit of weed out —a long thin bit like string. ' Give him another day and then we'll get to work,' he said.

" Well, I was completely hungry by that time, and weak too. But all I had to do was lie down and open my mouth.

" When Mark dropped the bit of weed down my throat I nearly bit it off and chewed it. But Mark had warned me about that, so I didn't bother.

" But frog did. I could feel him churning about, sniffing at the weed and making an effort to reach it. That was where Mark's cunning came in. As soon as I lifted my finger to tell him frog was moving he pulled the weed up an inch or two and I felt frog move up by the same amount.

" It was easy after that. Inch by inch Mark pulled the weed up until at last I could feel frog sitting just here where my Adam's apple is. Then Mark gave the final tug and pulled the weed out; and out jumped frog after it, right onto my chest. He made a plop like a cork as he came out, and there he sat, thin as a needle, poor little creature."

" Well, I took him back to the river and there he is to this day. We meet sometimes and he looks at me and I look at him. But there's no ill-feeling between us."

Robinson rose now and moved off. " Good day to you," he said.

When he had gone Harold said, " Lord! What a yarn."

Almost tentatively Doris said, " I suppose it *could* be true. I mean, it sounds feasible, really."

" Not when you consider that a frog's a cold-blooded creature and wouldn't live in a warm-blooded human."

But he wasn't really convinced. It *could* be true . . . couldn't it? He took out his pipe and filled it, puzzling But once he'd got it alight he lay back among the blue gentians, watching the sunlight shimmer on Doris' hair, the leaves of the poplars trembling against the sky, the slow ecstatic movement of a distant cornfield. That was true all right. This was no time to be bothering about the truth of a yarn. In three weeks they were going to be married : that was true, wasn't it? For a whole month they were going to be happy, just as they were happy now. That was true, wasn't it? "This is happiness," he said softly, thinking of the money he'd paid for it. And that was true.

Wasn't it?

VII

"YOU can't get away from the truth," Tom Prospect said. "Didn't I always say it was a nutty idea? Didn't I?"

Walt Earley nodded. Morrie Werner said, "You said that all right, Tom."

"And there it is in the paper. You can't get away from a leading article, can you?"

"Not from a leader, Tom. No."

The paper lay on the desk. It was an elaborate, expensive desk, copied from a design Prospect had seen in *Fortune*. It was an executive's desk, Honduras mahogany with inset bands of silver to give it tone. It had an automatic heater to warm the executive feet, a disappearing cocktail compartment, a streamlined dictaphone, a tray fitted out with manicure requisites and clothes brushes, a series of glass buttons to summon a series of secretaries. It was the ideal thing and it stood in the ideal office in the ideal building. Plate glass, solid silver ashtrays, air-conditioning, thermostatically-controlled heating. The staff deserved the best, the public deserved to see that they got it. Once a week parties were conducted round the Prospect building free of charge. Schoolchildren, suburban literary societies, chambers of commerce, rotarians, Darby-and-Joan clubs— all grand people, the backbone of business. They went away with literature—art-paper pamphlets, a booklet of testimonials, a toy cut-out book for the kids, coloured reproductions of the Institute of Hygiene's certificate pertaining to the cleanliness of Prospect-Before-You kitchens, the free tooth-beaker with PROSPECT HAPPINESS IS REAL HAPPINESS printed on it.

"And there's the truth staring everyone in the face," Prospect said. He pressed one of the glass buttons. A secretary came in. Werner and Earley stood up. Prospect insisted on manners in his staff. The girl sat down and crossed her knees. She shimmered—hair, lips, nails. Earley and Werner sat down in unison and with the same choreographic precision flicked lighters to the gold-tipped cigarette Prospect now put in his mouth. "Arrange to have reprints made of this leader. Fifty—no, a hundred thousand." The secretary went and returned in a few minutes with a brief letter. She laid it precisely on the gold-initialled blotting pad and departed once more. Carefully Prospect read the letter and pressed another button. This time it was a dark girl who came. "Signature," Prospect said. The dark girl smiled with a toothpaste gleam and stood holding a rocker blotter as Prospect signed. She blotted the signature and took the letter, holding it as if her fingers were tweezers, the letter a piece of boiling lint.

"Don't tell me I haven't got everything buttoned up." Prospect held the black cigarette between his smoothly cold-creamed fingers and looked down with bland pleasure at the ash curling whitely away.

Earley and Werner nodded. They took up the paper and read the leading article aloud, alternate paragraphs, like the chorus in an expressionist play.

"'This newspaper has always been in favour of progress, security and happiness. The words are given in that order deliberately, for a couple of years ago that would have been their natural order; and there are still very strong grounds for thinking that any interference with the natural order of things is unwise.' " And now Earley:

" ' MR. MOUNTALBAN'S discovery has meant revolution; and revolution in abstract things like progress, security and happiness is sufficiently near forbidden ground to be disturbing.' " Then Werner:

" ' No sane newspaper would deny that MR. MOUNT-ALBAN has benefited humanity. His was a noble gesture made for the common good. But like all humanitarian benefits, it is open to abuse.' " And Earley:

" ' It is useless to deny that the furtive vendors of forged and stolen tickets for HAPPYLAND are doing good business and causing grave disorder on the island, or that the national advertising campaign, coupled with that most potent of all forms of advertising—word-of-mouth recommendation—has created a demand which MR. MOUNT-ALBAN is finding it hard to cope with. It is also pertinent now to remind everyone—particularly H.M. MINISTER OF DEFENCE—that we have not yet found the X-bomb target.' " And Werner again:

" ' This weapon, on which our national security may depend, has not yet been tried. It is an unknown quantity. It exists, we know—so much we have been told by a government understandably anxious to preserve peace at all costs save the cost of appeasement. But will it work? Will this most terrible of all weapons inspire more than taunts in the hearts of potential enemies if they believe we are merely bluffing and own no weapon more effective than A- and H-bombs? And if they called our bluff, what then?' " And Earley:

" ' No, we are bluffing ourselves if we can command no knowledge of the efficiency of our Damocletian sword.' " And Werner:

" ' The weapon must be tried. And it must be tried here

93

in our own waters. So far the government has failed to find any alternative target. It is a bitter thing to say, but we are driven to it by the thought of consequences too awful to ponder, so we say boldly: *in the last resort even Happiness must be sacrificed to the needs of progress and security.*' " And Earley once more:

" ' Let the government stop dithering and face the fact: a target must be found, the X-bomb must be tried. If its effect is truly as the physicists claim, then we need be afraid no more. If not, then we must press on with its development.' " And now Werner, finally:

" ' But first—the target. We would remind the government that they once had the chance to purchase Happyland. They fumbled it. In a sense we were the gainers: we gained happiness—or, rather, a place where happiness could be bought. But what shall it profit a man if he gain happiness and lose his own security?' "

Werner put the paper down. His thin, handsome Hebraic face was composed and serious in the manner of a man who has been inspired by great and gloomy rhetoric. "That's good stuff that last bit."

Prospect rose and went to an alcove beside the pink glass fireplace. There the tiny daschund lay coiled in a lined basket. He lifted it and cradled it in his arms. " I'm glad you noticed that, Morrie. I like some classical intelligence in my personal assistants. That last bit's a—a—" He pressed one glass button, then another. A third secretary came in—a youngish man with a big nose and rimless glasses. At the same time a small jockey-type man in a long white overall entered. Prospect handed him the dog, carefully. " See if he wants to spend a penny." The overalled man went out, backwards, like a lord chamberlain in a pantomime, carrying the dog. Prospect said to the other man, " What did I tell you that was—that last bit of that leader?"

"A paraphrase, Mr. Prospect. On the biblical quotation ' What shall it profit a man if he gain— ' "

"That's all right. I remember now. You can go." Prospect opened the monogrammed cigarette box. Faintly the Prospect Jollity Song tinkled from its inside. "Sometimes I don't remember these things. Never try to remember everything, Morrie. Nor you, Walt."

"Sure not," Earley said admiringly.

"But remember some things."

"Of course. The important things, Tom," Werner said.

"Like me saying Happyland was a nutty idea right at the start. Bound to lead to trouble. And look where we are now : even bits in the papers about it."

"You were dead right," Werner said.

"As usual," Earley said.

Prospect lifted a finger. "I shan't want you boys no more today. I've got a lunch date—heavy."

His date was with the Minister, but he didn't tell anybody that. He took a taxi to the Minister's house in the desiccated part of Chelsea. The Minister chose to live there because his tastefully renovated and carefully tended house shone with jewelish opulence in the shrivelled square with its cracked windows and neglected trees.

"My dear fellow," the Minister said, taking Prospect from the butler, his monocle down-glinting at the inert daschund.

"He'll be no trouble, Minister. Stays in my arms the whole time. Or on my lap."

The interior of the Minister's house was very masculine. His wife had deserted him years before for a beautician's business in New York-Hollywood-Paris. There was no rancour between them. Occasionally she sent him letters beginning "Dear Toogles" and enclosing cheques as advance payments for his suggestions for suitable brand names for her new line in men's toiletries. " Something thoroughly masculine, dearest Toogles. That's why I come to you." The Minister wrote down names like Harris, Maddox, Buccaneer, Sundowner and the like and sent them off by air mail. But he didn't know if they ever got used. The cheques came in useful for paying his wine merchant.

Giving Prospect a drink the Minister said, " Business good?"

" Wonderful, wonderful. And of course I can handle all I get."

" A sly dig at Mr. Mountalban, eh?" The Minister looked sideways with histrionic meaning : " We know, my dear fellow, don't we?"

" I said from the first it was a nutty idea. I mean happiness—people were bound to rush for it. Demand bigger than supply : that situation always has created a corner, always will. Only the other day in the Savoy grill a man offered me a couple of fortnights in Happyland—even showed me the tickets." He looked with supercilious amusement at his reflection in the mirror.

The Minister began to laugh, standing straddle-legged with his hand on his hip. The sound was carefully controlled, mellow, well-bred yet hearty. " You! That's good : O! that's very good indeed! I must tell the P.M." He swilled his glass round as he considered the form the telling would take. ' One of Prospect's own men offered him a ticket for Happyland in the Savoy grill.' He visualised the P.M. tapping his *pince-nez* on his palm as he said, ' We must be careful, very careful, over this matter of Happyland. A word of warning to Prospect might not be amiss.'

" You know," he said at luncheon, " I can't help feeling we should have no qualms at all over helping, as it were behind the scenes, the public's clamour for a spell of happiness. I foresee that in a year or so—perhaps less—the situation out there will be beyond Mountalban's handling. And in a matter affecting the public he'll have to seek the government's co-operation. I don't see that we need have any qualms about bringing about th—er—inevitable end with the utmost expedition. Do you?"

"When Happyland's fall-down's going to bring me business?"

"No. But we must be careful. For your sake—for all our sakes."

"I'm being careful all right."

The Minister ran a careful hand over the polished segments of his hair. "And—always assuming that we wanted to—do you think we could expedite an ultimate—er—chaos in Happyland?"

"You mean could we do it quicker?"

"I do mean exactly that."

Prospect cut off a portion of peach, dipped it in cream and fed it to the dog. "It's like this, Minister: you ask for my advice—I give it to you. I ain't sure it'd be advisable to quick things up. Questions might get asked. The boys in my Psychology Div. tell me Mountalban's worried about coping with all the Happyland trippers. They're going, but they aren't coming back. Sleeping in cornfields and the like for the sake of whatever it is they find there. I've heard rumours. Before long it's going to be a sort of mass emigration."

The Minister said thoughtfully: "That means interference with industry. Of course we'd have to step in."

"It'd be best if you gave it its natural time and stepped in for the good of the people. See what I mean? If it appears like you're doing it for their sakes and not because you're poking your noses . . . see what I mean?"

"I understand perfectly, my dear fellow. You mean it's best if we act without precipitation, in the fulness of time."

97

Prospect offered his platinum cigarette case to the Minister. The Minister took one, though he hated cigarettes and knew this one would ruin the taste of the port.

"Unusual, eh? Black paper, see? I like being different to everyone else."

"They'd be excellent for funerals," the Minister said drily. He repeated the witticism later at Cradle's and got a laugh from a dutiful back-bencher.

"Of course," Prospect said, "I'd be keeping any fingers I might have in the pie . . . well, I'd be keeping them in. Any fingers I might have, I said. Such as fingers who might drop a word here and there, spread the idea that people ought to get shirty when they're refused bookings to Happyland."

"You know," the Minister said thoughtfully, "I was saying only the other day to the P.M. that you're one of our most able business men. It pleased me to think of you as a scion of commerce, as Lord Prospect, say—Baron Prospect of Elysium."

"Did it?" Prospect said without curiosity. "The press says you ought to get a move on and get this target buttoned up."

The Minister said with epigrammatic lightness: "The press is at once the friend and the enemy of every government."

"I thought the press was public opinion."

The Minister put his monocle to his eye. "The press encourages that sentiment, my dear fellow; probably initiated it. Public opinion at the moment is that it wants to buy Mr. Mountalban's — er — product. It has little interest in X-, Y- or Z-bombs. I don't know that I altogether blame it." He added sententiously: "But what people want isn't always what's best for them."

"Or for us either," Prospect said with sly joviality. As

98

he departed he said, as if the thought had just occurred to him: "That was a nice idea, that one you thought up —that Baron Prospect idea."

"Just a thought, my dear fellow; just a thought."

Prospect looked back from his taxi at the Minister watching him depart. 'He's a worried man.'

He returned to his office. "Charter me an air-taxi for Cleethorpes. Ring Transport Div and tell them to hold a boat for me—no, skip it, I'll go over with the regular trip. Always nice to see human beings, real good, simple people. I shan't want you or Morrie, Walt. I just got a yen to see people enjoying themselves the Prospect way."

"Isn't he a great feller?" Earley asked Werner.

"Ought to be raised to the peerage for all the good he's done mankind."

At the door Prospect turned. "You really think that, Morrie? I appreciate that. It's the warmth of human kindness."

Alone in space in the small aircraft he felt incredibly lonely. He'd brought jollity to millions of people and he ought to be just about the happiest man this side of the golden gate, wherever that was (he'd read of the place somewhere); but he felt lonely. 'I need a spell of Elysium. Maybe I'll stay up there a day or two.' He wasn't a one to mope. If the whole damn' world went for six in a shooting match there wasn't a thing he or anyone else could do to stop it. 'Cheer yourself up, Tom boy.' There'd be a girl or two floating loose-ended in some of the single bungies. There was always a girl or two. Chum up. Chum up with everybody. They lapped it up. It was good publicity. 'We had a fortnight at Elysium and Tom Prospect himself was there, joined in everything, the boss himself, took a girl or two about, well can you blame him? A man like that must have time on his hands and money to burn.' It made you

....MBERWE.
...BLIC LIBRARIE

feel like God. ' I'm Eric Mountalban's God all right,' he thought savagely. ' Him and his crazy Happyland. Going against nature, doing business that way. I'll smite him like in the Bible.'

He said to the pilot : " Where'd you go for your holiday, son ?"

The pilot turned his head. He was about twenty-two, with thick red hair and eyes at once curious and hopeful. " Where's everyone go nowadays? Elysium or Happyland. I tried a spot of Ha—"

" Did you like it, son ?"

" We were happy all right. I've been trying to puzzle out ever since why."

" I'll tell you," Prospect said. " When a man's paid for something he's swindled into believing's there, he won't ever admit he's been done brown as a toasted bun."

" No," the pilot said without animosity, as if he were reasoning with a child who had sinned and couldn't under-stand sin, " I think you're wrong there, sir. Have you actually been ?"

" To that place ? What the hell would I go there for ? I'm—"

" I know," the pilot said, still gently. " But you asked me. And it's true—what they say about happiness being there. I've got reasons for knowing it's true. Particular reasons. My bride and I . . . well, you find something there that isn't anywhere else in the world. Peace isn't handicrafts and folkweave and tootling on recorders round a maypole with folk dances, it's something positive. The way I worked it out's like this : it's the same as one of those nuns who go into convents, lie on six inches of planking with their hands folded on their flat chests all ready to lay out in case they die in the night, wearing a hair shirt all their lives and long-ing to be humiliated so they can suffer—I used to think

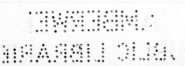

they were mad. But there's some sort of burning inside them that makes them do it. They can't explain it and nobody can understand it till they get the same burning. Well, it's the same thing with happiness. You've got to start with a bit of faith. You're really got to believe it exists like water or flowers or bricks and mortar; you've got to look with a new eye, as if you were just being taught from the beginning and didn't have any reason at all to think what people told you might be phoney. And once you do that you're all right. There's no going back." The pilot's voice ceased. The plane droned on over thin vaporous clouds. "But there's got to be a going back in another way: to everyday life. All the world's history of spilt blood and corruption's set in the blood. It kids you that valour and fortitude start at nine on Monday morning. 'That's life,' you tell yourself. 'I must be there to take part in it. Happiness is something we've learnt to do without or make for ourselves so we can do without it again, make it for ourselves again.' So we come back to our own piddling little jobs, kid ourselves we're serving mankind, kid ourselves there's happiness to be found in everything. Then we set out to smash the real thing up because we're afraid of it. That's what's happening; that's what's going to happen." His eyes were bright. He was like a child peering for the first time through a peephole on to the endless corrupted vistas of humanity. "You know what? It'll work out this way: there'll be millions made curious by the thousands that have been there; and because the millions have inherited a few aeons of democracy and whatever mad scheme people lived by before democracy, they'll want to achieve that happiness the few thousands tell them about, conquer it, have it—not because they've any kind of right to it but because they make themselves believe they've a right to it. And then they'll take it by force. And after that—because it isn't anything like ended yet—there'll be others, there'll be something, there'll be . . ." His voice faded like the voice of a child who has forgotten the lines of a verse he is reciting. "You know, I saw it then, the way it'll end, the—"

Prospect sat with the cigarette burned down to the gold tip, the smoke wisping with a faint tarry burn of nicotine across his lip, his mouth slightly open, as if astonishment pressed like two fingers on his cheeks. "I'd like to see the boys in my Psychology Div get to work on you. They know all about human nature. I pay 'em to know it. You'd be the bee's knees to them. They—"

But the pilot was speaking to the airport now. He had put on the rakish peaked cap of his uniform and had left his secret place at the peephole. 'He's a good-looking boy,' Prospect thought. 'You wouldn't ever think he was crackers.'

"We're going in," the pilot said. "We'll be on terra in five minutes."

When they landed Prospect said to the Elysium Welcoming Committee. "I'm incog this time—just want to have a quiz round."

He went over in the regular speedboat, forcing himself not to beam at everyone, thinking with pleasure of the difficulty of keeping himself unknown to people and wondering how long he could keep it up. There were two women and a man in the boat with him. One of the women was thin and sharp and wore the irrepressibly curious expression of a woman who spends the mornings of her life listening to conversations at adjoining tables in Cadenas and Kardomahs and will one day run her grandchildren's lives with the same inexorable stupidity that drives her own. The other woman was fat, sitting swathed and composed and slightly lopsided as the rake of the boat tipped her. She had a conjectural tone of voice and spoke slowly in bright shrieking drops like an incessant tap.

"You know, I think we ought to introduce ourselves. If there's one thing I hate it's a strained feeling." The boat's engine roared and her voice, fenced with its doll teeth, screeched on the sound and spray. "I'm Tina Mowbray—Miss—and this is Carol Good—Mrs."

"I'm sure I'm pleased to meet you," Prospect shouted. The engine suddenly cut out and his words hung in the air like insults. He felt himself flush. His embarrassment wasn't in any way connected with the women. He felt that the man who sat beside him—an insignificant man in decorous and unobtrusive black clothes, his ears and nose large, his spectacles thick—was in some way contemptuous; but when he looked there was nothing at all to take exception to in his manner. He was quite inoffensive. He was studying, with close attention, a catalogue of some kind.

"We're combining business with pleasure," Tina shrieked. Her words tore through noise and spray. "Up here . . . local lit'ry society . . . objective report . . . these wonderful holiday camps . . ."

He heard her voice tearing through the air and spray long after Elysium had clutched them with arms of jollity. Evidently the reception officer had passed on word to the camp, for no one acknowledged him. He had a single bungalow of the standard type and joined in everything. He had to. Somewhere behind him the peephole had opened and closed; he had glimpsed doom and wouldn't acknowledge it. He danced with Tina Mowbray and Carol Good in the vast girdered dance hall speared with searching spotlights and thumped by the purple-and-white-suited musicians' music with its sexual ecstasy compounded of C of E hymns and Haarlem flophouse songs.

From the shadows and the crowds Fitch watched—watched and listened.

Fitch sensed something. His bulging nose and myopic eyes had led him to Elysium. " I think there might be a thing or two to learn on our friend's island," he told Mr. Mountalban. " One hears *vox populi* in such places."

He returned two weeks later. " *Vox populi* is a terrible thing," he said, tapping the walnut desk behind which Mr. Mountalban watched with thin suburban petulance. " But not so terrible as *vox oceani*."

" Even if you were to speak in English riddles I might be able to make something of what I presume you have to say."

" The voice of the sea," Fitch said with glib pleasure. " A consuming, hungry voice. It demands, from the coastline up there, six inches every—"

" I hardly think," Mountalban said, " that your information is likely to be as reliable as mine for which I paid a big fee to an eminent geologist. He gave me *one* inch as the annual figure of erosion."

Fitch shrugged, pressed his hand to his chest. " Some times I feel things here. An inner voice of compulsion—"

" Your ulcer, doubtless," Mountalban said with bland levity. " In any case, the voice I am concerned with at the moment is the voice of the people."

" *Vox populi*. Yes." His sallow lips softly formed literary phrases : " It is the voice of unrest. People are troubled. Happiness—thanks to the genius of Mr. Mountalban—is theirs so long as they can pay for it. They have come to accept it as a commodity, like cheese or soap. They resent being told in your advertising that no new bookings can be accepted for the time being. They're like people—they *are* people—who have marched since the world's beginning toward the ultimate goal and now find that the goal is being gradually drawn away by ' they.' It isn't understood; and because it isn't understood it's bitterly resented. You can see it in people as they sit in buses and trains; you can see them thinking, ' Why should those who've had their share be allowed to stay on?' You couldn't convince them they'd act the same."

Mountalban said wearily: " Why can't they be patient? I explain over and over again—"

" Fifty millions in this country. Space is a deceiving thing, but it isn't elastic. I daresay you could get fifty millions on Happyland, shoulder to shoulder, packed like sardines "—as he said the word he felt the reactionary heartburn in his throat—" but it wouldn't end there. Because all the world's looking on, standing aside now, but waiting their time. Black, white, yellow and red humanity —they all learn, whatever language they speak, that there's a word in it that means ha—"

" You're quite a philosopher, Mr. Fitch. But I pay you for information only. What have you heard, what do you actually know?"

" Heard? Know? Ah! so many things. That the *marché noir* in tickets for Happyland is a flourishing concern; that it is probably—I say probably—organised by a certain person; that the evening paper has it that there are twenty-three thousand people in addition to the static population on the island of Happyland at this moment—"

Mountalban glanced down at a typed slip of paper stuck in the corner of his blotter. " For a newspaper that's an accurate figure. Only six thousand out."

" —that the press is trying to swing opinion away from the thought of Happiness to the thought of Security; and that the cartoonists and versifiers and fictioneers are making hay while the sun shines. They have the gift of vision, you know. I can understand it: I have it myself, but not the means of expressing it. They're saying that there's going to be a blow-up." He laid his finger alongside his nose. "A blow-up. But what *sort* of a blow-up, eh? That's the point, eh?"

Mr. Mountalban looked across the desk at Fitch. Behind him in the corner the tape entrails of the news machine unwound themselves ceaselessly. Witwatersrand, Consolidated. Minor disturbance in Coventry Street—

He felt Fitch breathing over his shoulder. "You see— it's already started." He turned about in his mind for an appropriate thought. "No smoke without fire."

He went on to tell Mr. Mountalban unimportant details of his visit to Elysium. "Tom Prospect's up there—was, rather. He looked afraid. Afraid of what? I asked myself. Sheltering in the charms of two women." Fitch gave a delicate shudder. "Oh, those women. They lured Prospect to what was called a concert. I sat behind them and the thin one knitted the whole time—something long and brown, a comfort for a troop somewhere perhaps." He shuddered again as he recalled the smoke-laden hall with its thousands of constantly changing lights, illuminated Wurlitzer and usherettes in green uniforms. A woman had played an attenuated version of the Grieg piano concerto. She flashed with *diamanté*—a scraggy woman in a girlish dress and with a mouthful of very false teeth, her hair piled elaborately. She stormed and sweated at the piano and took a bow, in a purple spotlight and a thunder of applause, looking exactly like the manageress of a cheap dress shop after a row with a customer. "It was dreadful—dreadful. And the thin knitting woman was whispering to Prospect all the time—telling him how the knitted thing was to be raffled in a jumble sale to get funds for the New Hurtleford Literary and Debating Society. Then the other one, the fat

106

one, told him how she was up there trying to get an objective viewpoint to write an article on Happiness for the Hurtleford *Gazette*. She kept saying, ' We must have both points of view. In a democracy it's essential that we have both points of view.' And all the time that awful woman was pounding away at the piano. I felt ill—ill.''

Mr. Mountalban sat down at the desk again. Fitch's voice droning on and on, Fitch feeling ill because a scraggy woman was massacring the Grieg concerto, a thin woman was knitting, a fat woman was talking about democracy; Fitch listening and watching, Fitch going everywhere and letting the scraps of information impinge on him and stick like particles of dust; Fitch imbibing conversaton as a leech imbibes blood, swelling with it, bursting with it, leaving himself empty and dissolute, a bladder deflated. It was a sound at once importunate and welcome, the voice of a cringing beggar who returns a priceless possession and bargains for its release. Mountalban didn't want to stop Fitch talking. ' Fitch, you are my friend, my only friend, We understand each other.'

He let Fitch's voice uncoil while the tape ticked remorselessly in its corner. Minor disturbance in Coventry Street. A small group of people had threatened the booking assistant with violence if she didn't guarantee a family booking to Happyland for the middle weeks of September. It had been put under control very quickly, a passing policeman's voice had quelled it; but it had happened. Mountalban knew all the pointers to trouble. He knew them so well. They had cropped up all along his life and he'd dealt with them—pushed them out of sight or thrust them down. Novelties Ltd., Neon Arcades, Consolidated Milk Mars, even steel and houses and aircraft corporations—they had all spelled their own kind of trouble; but to do something for the good of humanity in expiation of dubious achieve-

ments and still to be beaten—he thought of it as unfair.
'Too many things against me.'

But they were all things he directed himself: his companies controlled the manufacture of X-bomb plants, houses
for workers, the garish cars they rode in, the literature they
read, the ice-cream they licked, the joke novelties they
amused each other with, the aeroplanes they rode to foreign
lands in, the other aircraft in which lay security in the
pressure of a button. Involvement grew up like a forest.
'But Happiness is the greatest thing I've ever given them,
the greatest thing anybody has ever given anyone.' He'd
despised Creech for being afraid, but now he was afraid
himself. 'I've given them too much, perhaps that's it.' He
avoided seeing that whichever way it went now he could
no longer lose: he controlled too much. Fitch would have
said: 'What you lose on the swings you gain on the round-
abouts.'

"Are you all right?" Fitch said suddenly. "You look a
little peaky." He brought out the little bakelite box. "Take
one of these in a glass of hot water. They're such a relief."
Mountalban raised his hand. "No. I'm disappointed,
weary, lonely." The thin clerkly voice was precise, clear; it
might have been reading from a company report. "I give
people Happiness and they abuse it, they fight among
themselves for possession of it, they can't bear to return
to the life they belong to. Why can't they realise it must—
it *must*—be a temporary thing, something to take like a
holiday, once a year. Why must they turn it into something
to be possessed, like . . . like money?"

He crossed to the window, stood looking out, stood listening to Fitch making little sucking noises, Fitch getting ready
to be on his way again. "Why do they do that?"

"I don't know. I don't know. Nobody knows. Everybody
knows. Everybody knows why it happens in somebody else,

but never knows why it happens in himself. It's something to do with human nature."

"That's right," Mountalban said, remembering how he had thought of himself as the Apostle of the Simple Life. "Human nature."

VIII

BRUTUS Robinson spoke of Harold and Doris. "They tell me the two weeks they've been here have been two hours."

De Montfort nodded as at an oft-repeated phrase. "More and more come, fewer and fewer leave—for that very reason. The ships go back half empty. After all, they can't drag people off."

The burnished heat of afternoon dimmed a little over the island. It was not so much a lessening of light and heat as an infinitesimal pause in time—as though time actually stood still and within its pause the island watched itself breathe, live, reflect.

"On the way to evening," de Montfort said. He didn't speak with regret, nor with great pleasure either, though the phrase had its own significance. His deep voice might have been a kind of designation of time in a place where all clocks had run down—and in fact there were very few clocks on the island; certainly no accurate ones, except the watches of visitors who had wound them with automatic repetition night and morning, regardless now of loss or gain.

"Harold Bassett's is a fine watch," de Montfort said now. "Hands and dials and places to tell the day and what month and whether the moon's round or crescent." His voice did not betray the fact that he could see no use for such an instrument.

Brutus Robinson set his wine down on the table. He broke a piece of the coarse bread of the island and dipped it in the wine. The drops were bright in the sun, purple; each drop had the sheen, the purple lustre, of sloes. Sunlight glinted all through the room—on pewter, copper, resined lute-strings, the long refectory table which for upward of seven hundred years had been waxed daily in a succession of movements as regular and unrelenting as the sun reflected in the surface.

" Odd. Like human nature." It was a reflection Robinson might have made years earlier, before he came to the island. It meant nothing to de Montfort or Judith Prince or Janet Tiptree or Mark Bickmore. (They were all there; but it couldn't be said that they were gathered there: it was simply that chance and tasks and perhaps desire had drawn them together there in that room in *The Lute Player*—just as it might have brought them together in a hundred other places on the island : without deliberation, or at least more of it than sufficed to direct their feet in one direction rather than another.) It meant very little even to Brutus Robinson himself now : it was simply that the words had spoken themselves, as for no reason at all a man will repeat some child- or youth-phrase that he believes he has long since forgotten. " Yes. Odd."

" He's a man bothered about something, I'd say." De Montfort stood with both palms pressing on the table. Sunlight on the yellow bars of his waistcoat, behind them his huge breathing—regular, gentle; but huge. " It could be time that bothers him."

" There was a time when I was time," Brutus Robinson said, wine glistening on his lips. " I was responsible for taking a clock round and round a factory, in the dead of night, for the sake of recording, on coloured tickets, the time the clock said."

Judith Prince took an apple from her pocket and bit into it. The beaded juice glistened like sweat along the line of her lip. " But if the clock was there in your hand—?"

" It's a long story. It has to do with the time I was put in charge of a place that made time. There used to be a saying people said to each other, especially children : ' You haven't got time? Well, make time.' This was the place where they made it. And I—" He told them the story. Thomas Loomes came in halfway through and stood listening. Later when he saw Robinson alone he said, " You're the biggest liar that ever walked," and Robinson said, " It's a story. Everybody enjoys a story." But now, when the story was finished, nobody said anything for a moment. They received it in silence and pleasure, as a story should be received. Then Janet Tiptree said :

" I think it's not time that bothers him, but marriage. He knows everything and he knows nothing. And the nothing bothers him."

" It may be that," Mark Bickmore said. He was old and tall and wore turtleneck sweaters; summer and winter he wore turtleneck sweaters; always three—red, yellow and green, in that order, the green outermost. " It may be a sort of shyness. When do you marry them, Thomas Loomes?"

" In a week—if I can get into the church. So many people here now—they come to look and stay to pray—as if they're making up for years and years of not praying : row upon row of them, even in the aisles and chancel. They enjoy themselves."

" It seemed strange at first—I mean the crowds." Judith Prince picked up her basket. " But I'm used to them now. They might have been here always. Goodbye all."

" If you want solitude," de Montfort said, " here in the afternoon is your place. It seems they're used to certain hours for the wine-bibbing and the habit sticks."

Loomes and Robinson left *The Lute Player* and walked together out of the village. " We were talking of Harold Bassett," Robinson said.

" So we were. Is there more to say?"

" Not now. I see him and his girl coming along the road. He looks at her as if he wants to lick his lips but doesn't because he thinks it wouldn't be very gentlemanly. But there's nothing he'd like better than to have someone dig him in the ribs and call him a wolf. Yet to be given the chance to play wolf—that'd be a very different thing."

" It's the prerogative of all vulgarians to be shocked." Loomes dug the epigram up from somewhere, but there was no malice in his tone.

Harold and Doris stopped and waited for Loomes and Robinson to approach them. Doris wore the same cotton dress in which she had arrived. She had washed and pressed it daily, washing it at midday as though she had no other garment to wear (though there were in fact three more dresses in the tan fibre case beneath the bed) and holding it out of her bedroom window for perhaps ten minutes while the midday sun dried it, standing at the open window in her underclothes—as though she would vouchsafe her desire just this much exhibitionism and no more—and thinking that perhaps Harold might be walking in the orchard and see her and show by his scanty attention that he was neither shocked nor more than passingly interested, like the artists and sculptors who had models posing for them daily and took not a bit of notice, so she'd heard (though of course one didn't know what to believe). She could have worn any one of her other three dresses, but she chose to wash and wear only the one daily for the sake of the midday routine. She had told Harold with slight archness that she did this, but she didn't know whether he watched. Certainly she could have asked him: but it was pleasanter to suppose that he acted 'like a man.'

"Hullo," Harold Bassett said. He too wore the same clothes—the tan slacks and cerise linen shirt; but he had discarded the jacket. His manner and gestures were the same—respectable yet insouciant, assured yet only spuriously so—but it was as if something else had been added, had grown round—as if happiness had taken him by surprise in spite of his professed expectations, and had found him watchful rather than receptive. He had now more than ever the air of a man who watches himself. He carried a copy of *Punch* and some newspapers. "I collected them from the wagon that brought a new party into Sumer."

"The manse will be getting somewhat crowded," Loomes said. "But no doubt we shall manage."

It was not only the manse: every house in every village and hamlet had more than enough people to feed and shelter. When the time came for people to return they walked to parts of the island farthest from the harbour. The captains of the ships that should have picked them up had their instructions: after a while they began to cruise round the island at a half-mile's distance from the shore, anchor and despatch longboats to pick up parties for England. But people just gathered there until the longboat was a few hundred yards from the shore and then went back inland. It was not the instinct of mutiny or wilfulness that provoked them; it was simply a kind of mass decision taken without reference either to each other or to any spoken idea, as if no reasoned explanation was necessary. After a while the ships took off the few who, either because they could not make the effort of will or because even happiness

H

could not overcome their reasons for returning, were waiting on the quay, and didn't bother to cruise round the island. The captain of one of them said: " I'm a ship's captain, not a wet nurse." His second officer said: " You wouldn't think so many of them would be willing to part from their families—even for happiness." The captain explained: " They send for them. Those that can't get genuine tickets, phoney tickets or any other kind of tickets —they charter boats to bring 'em out. There's no stopping 'em when they really want to do something."

It was in fact becoming a minor invasion. The desire to possess happiness had infected people. They didn't reason, they became inflamed. It was the gold rush over again, but with a difference: no man was disappointed.

Harold Bassett, carrying in his hand the newspapers from England and his pipe carefully encircled by thumb and forefinger, said with deliberation: " I've just seen a landmark—a landmark in history as well as on the island: a family down in the valley are building a house. It's a shack—just wood and mud and leaves; but it's significant. It's the first one."

Loomes nodded. " Yes. Significant." He looked away across the fields, bright now in the imminent copper glow of early evening. His voice as he spoke was musing, gentle, entirely without rhetoric or even dramatic inflexion. He might have been summarising to himself as he stood alone in his vestry the points of a sermon that might offer food for thought: " Yes: significant as the first arrivals in any land are significant, because they bring new ideas, a new language, a new concept of living, But in this case significant in another way: because here there is nothing they can impose on our way of life, because they are spellbound. Yes: spellbound."

He paused. The sound of people laughing came from

close at hand. They came in sight—a crowd of perhaps forty, coming up out of the fields with flowers. Loomes waved and the others waved, and passed on.

" Until a while ago," Loomes continued now, " all the generations of this place had been balanced in numbers by birth, and death—balanced naturally, without any decision on anybody's part, so that its economy was balanced too. Now things must be different: not badly different, but different: there is the same space, but more humanity to partake of it."

" Lebensraum," Harold Bassett said; but nobody understood what he meant.

He and Doris and Loomes and Robinson walked together through Bluecopse and through the vineyard and up across the hills to Sumer. There were many people now where before every step might have been taken in solitude—not a surging of bodies as in a crowd, but a sense of the presence of larger numbers than could actually be seen, as if for every man, woman or child or group of men, women and children whom one passed and saw in actual physical fact there was an equal or greater number nearby. It was an awareness of great numbers made manifest by the same token as a deserted house or street or city will imply its emptiness by neither evidence nor proof—since every curtain may be billowing as at windows newly opened for the morning and every garden freshly turned and every clock on each mantelshelf wound and accurate, and still the place may be as unpeopled as a sea-sunk village.

" You feel the place filling up," Loomes mused. " Like a hall before a concert."

They came to the manse. It was a grey stone house of twelve rooms, in the smallest of which Loomes lived alone, sleeping on a truckle bed and with no other furnishings but a table, a chair and some shelves with books. From there they looked across a wild shrubbery and an arbour of flowering magnolias and casuarinas to the summit where stood the Earl's mansion house, peopled now with those whom he had wanted to serve.

"There's the news," Harold Bassett said. He put the papers down on the table, looking at them with an air of mild puzzlement, as if he could not quite believe that he was concerned in the news they contained. "News from a far country."

It was all there—unrest in two-inch headlines,

In an interview with our Special Correspondent Mr. Smollett said with the true determination of the English working man: " If there's Happiness to be had my family and I are as much entitled to it as anyone else. I resented it when we were refused book-ings to Happyland and I let myself go. I regret being uncivil to the young lady, but I think I was justified, witticisms in Mr. Punch's Charivaria, *Happiness is in short supply, we're told. How short, O Lord, how short?* explanation in the advertisement columns, *Please be patient. We are doing all we can to cope with the right-minded but phenomenal demand, but for the good of the country's economy we beg your indulgence. We must, for a little while longer, ration your period of Happiness. Remember—there are others besides you. And please avoid the black market in forged and stolen Happyland warrants as you would the plague. The government is introducing legislation that will deal adequately with offenders in this respect, so this request is in the nature of a warning.*

Harold Bassett pointed with his pipe at the paper. "Queer it should make such a stir." But his own puzzle-ment troubled him a little. Faintly as in a reminiscence he heard himself question with intentional deliberation : ' And why do people stay on, refuse to return?' and the question that would answer the question: ' Will you yourself return when the time comes?' But it was a thought only, it was as faint as his memory of Soho audition rooms, Tschaikowski concerts in the girdered echoic spaces of Harringay, the note posted at Paddington for the parents left alone. The memories were clear but without depth, there was no illusion of perspective. Only happiness had perspective, reality, now.

" Over there," Brutus Robinson said, tapping the paper with his wrinkled finger, " there are two realities it seems." He smoothed back the hairlessness of his high forehead. " The happiness; the bomb. Two factions. Two factions means a disagreement; a disagreement means a disturbance; a disturbance—"

Doris touched Harold's arm. They went quietly out of the house. In the quiet places there was no longer any solitude: people stood and walked in groups and by the river there were many who fished with nets scooping the water between two boats. " You see? Wherever people are they've got to think of food and shelter. I spoke to some this morning who've staked a claim. They just put a stick in the ground and drew a circle round it."

They entered a copse and for a moment they were alone. Doris stood still. " How are we . . . I mean, shall we want to go back?" It was a question that didn't really belong.

" I don't know."

All the rest of the dreaming afternoon they walked on the island, from village to village. Everyone seemed to know that they were going to be married. " It's like a plot."

" Against us?" Doris asked.

" Not against us. Just a plot; as if they're all determined to take part in it, I mean the wedding, somehow."

" That's ever so nice. It's the way people are at home,

standing about outside the church, perfect strangers, ready to throw rose petals, wish you luck. That's taking part really."

It wasn't what Harold Bassett meant, but he didn't say anything. It didn't seem necessary.

But he was right all right. There was something that went with the islanders' happiness: they had a sense of humour individually droll and collectively mischievous, possibly even mildly libidinous—it would certainly be considered so by that section of society typified for Harold by the Cheesmans and by his own parents and brothers and by the philistines against whom he imagined himself in revolt. But it wasn't altogether obvious, " nor transferable either," Robinson once said in a conversation with Loomes. (They were always conversing, these two, their status as immigrants setting them a little apart, giving them a common viewpoint which had begun by being a defence— since they, equally with the immigrants of a score of years later, brought their inherent antagonism of despondency and suspicion—and had become in less time than either of them had been aware of a mere excuse for calling on each other so that each could observe how in the other despondency and suspicion had quickly died and discuss the reason therefor, with ever-decreasing interest as their happiness grew. But the common factor of their immigration remained; and their particular friendship remained too— heritage of days when it might have been needed as a bulwark).

So when the time came the islanders' mischief took its own course.

It happened that two evenings before the wedding Judith Prince came into *The Lute Player* at dusk. No candles had yet been lit and the shadowy figures of those present, and their voices, low and insistent, were like ghosts of old departed humours in the room—as if in anticipation of what she was about to say they had conjured whispers of a sly wickedness at once saturnine and disarming.

"Thomas Loomes has had to go to bed. A bit of a fever and his legs are weak under him."

Immediately the room took on a different air. De Montfort, with a long taper to the candles in their silver sconces, stepped back from the nimbus of light and handed the taper to Robinson. Then he took wine and stone jars of herbs and mortar and pestle and began to manufacture an anodyne. Without anything being said everyone's concern was implicit. Harold Bassett, coming downstairs from his room just at that moment, with his pipe in his mouth and a book under his arm, said anxiously, "But it's only thirty-six hours to the time he's to marry us."

"He can marry you in bed as well as anywhere else," Robinson said as he pinched the taper and watched the curl of smoke fade among the beams. "If he's still there, that is."

Nobody thought it likely he would be. But it chanced that twenty-four hours later he was in a coma. Somewhere, years before he had come to the island, there'd been an onslaught of malaria in his life and it had chosen to reassert itself just now.

"He's lying there sweating himself to a shadow and shivering so much the books fall down off the shelves, almost," Janet Tiptree said to Doris.

"What can we do?" Doris wanted to know; but her concern was not wholly spontaneous : its impulse was in a way conventional, redolent of the neighbourly attitude of quickly-brewed tea to relieve Mrs. Next-door's distress in a minor crisis. And pumping her heart quickly now was an even stronger concern. "Our wedding," she whispered, almost as if she spoke to herself.

Beyond the window dusk again burdened the orchard, the faint sound of singing came from somewhere in the village, and beyond that again was the heavy scented silence of the island. Across Doris's concern the reminiscence of lush romantic technicolour sprang and she trembled in awareness of her vulgarity. It was as if in the sharpness of her happiness was a measure of apprehension, as if the burden of terraced houses with tool-sheds and amateur rockeries, and glasses of ginger wine sipped with daring aplomb in panelled saloon lounges lingered yet; and she spoke out with something of the old inherent fear of whispered gossip, but masked by the island's spell and the natural archness of her character: " I don't see how we're going to manage. You'll want the room." She flushed and looked down as she thought of the planned double bed on the morrow, the fight against embarrassment in the room in which she was certain Harold would want the light on as they undressed, the tendency to giggle against which she already battled. With a not-quite-genuine horror she said: " But now . . . what if we can't get married?"

" I must have the room," Janet Tiptree said. " With the crowds promised accommodation . . . four coming in here." Embracing innocence and innuendo at the same time she added: " Of course it was arranged from the beginning you'd share room and bed at de Montfort's as from to-morrow night."

" But if we can't get *married*—"

Ignoring the shocked wonder, perhaps even sponsoring its defeat, the elder woman said simply: " Listen."

And into the middle of that silence the sound of a romantic song came. Possibly it was sung by one of the four who the next day might occupy this room. " Two other pairs of lovers. They want a wire stretched across the room and blankets hung. That will make it into two rooms, they think. Perhaps you could do the same with your man?"

" No, no." Horror's inflexion was audible now. " In the same room . . .? I mean . . ."

Janet Tiptree spoke now with softly sly amusement that she sensed at once would remain undetected : " The moral certainty is that the room is bespoken."

Repeating the moral certainty to Harold as they said goodnight in the copse of poplars whose every leaf seemed to rustle with the ascending whispered chorus of other lovers' valedictions, she heard him say stoically : " He may be better tomorrow. Miracles happen in this place. I went over with Brutus Robinson to see him and the fever seemed to have toned down a bit. He just looked yellow with the quinine and a bit weak. But anyway—" the stoicism, oddly, was unwelcome and without assurance; and she caught the echo of an old suburban wish for him to be a bit less intelligent, in a way—" but anyway, whatever happens . . . it'll be *all right*. Get me?"

" Of course." She had always ' got him.' He put himself over. He needed a little mild responsibility and she gave it to him, gladly, almost unwittingly, so that she might enjoy his pleasure, suffer herself to be ' mastered ' the true traditional male way. " You know I trust you, Hal. Whatever you said to do—"

His pipe glowed and somewhere nearby a few twigs rustled as with a shifting weight. " Even that." His voice was approving. " But of course it won't be necessary. To— er—succumb for the sake of succumbing is as bad as to withhold from the—er—final act because traditional morality says you must. We're creatures of free will."

" Of course," she said again. " And anyway we're crossing bridges. The parson may be better tomorrow. Better enough to say the words to us at his bedside anyway."

The scene took on its glow of romanticism again in her imagination; but she suspected it had little chance of fulfilment.

She was right. " Thomas Loomes is poorly yet." The villagers' faces were grave but not sad : it was the gravity of sympathy rather than regret; their compassion was for pain, not death.

Harold and Doris went into Sumer. The manse was still and all round people were being quiet; but although he was a loved man there were no tears. " We'll have to go : he's in the coma still, or maybe it's just sleep." The two went from the room. " Strange how you don't feel any resentment here : at home we'd have felt bitter, disappointed."

" We just know it'll be all right," she said, clutching his hand. " But tonight . . . I don't know about tonight."

He was quite unaware that he looked down at her with a kind of spurious tender manliness—a Code of Honour look that would have made him scream with laughter, seeing it on someone else's face. ' Boy Scout battling with Dragon Dirtythought '—he'd even have found a name for it. " Tonight'll be all right." He even patted her hand.

While he was patting it Janet Tiptree was patting down the peach satin nightie in the fibre suitcase. " There : everything of hers is in there."

" And'll stay there—tonight, anyway." De Montfort picked up the case. " A pity. I always look forward to the sounds of love."

" We may persuade him yet," Janet Tiptree said, watching de Montfort take the suitcase four doors along the village street, hearing enacted in her mind the quite sessions of love.

But there was no persuading him. Resolutely he bade Doris goodnight among the poplars. Even in the darkness she let her glance fall shyly downward as she thought with remote urgency of Bunce's eyes bright with tears and his whispered middle-aged thought—"You're so very beautiful." But here in Happyland it lacked the furtive appeal of eager revelation.

"Goodnight, Hal. We've still . . . still got it to look forward to." She said it with genuine happiness. The thrill for which she had deserted Daphne, thumbed her nose at convention in terrace houses for ever, drawn on an immense store of courage she was astonished at possessing, in order to make a dramatic exit—it was being drawn gently away from her. Of course it was Kismet; Kismet being a tease.

"The only thing is," she asked, "where will you sleep tonight."

"Me?" Stoicism popped out again like the quotations from Eliot and Pound that were beyond his comprehension but always seemed to impress other people. "De Montfort'll give me a shakedown somewhere."

The shakedown was in the attic above Doris's bedroom. Apples were stored there, the scent of them filled the darkness as he lay thinking of Doris. De Montfort's head, illumined by the candle he held, had sunk with slow deliberation through the trap. "She's beneath you"—and he closed one eye; there was no denying the implication. 'Of course he thinks I'm that type. I suppose most of the chaps here are. Anything for a bit of copulation.'

It sickened him a little even to consider it; but desire was there in the smell of the apples, the pricking of his flesh, the knowledge that Doris was lying sleepless too, that she would accept him—he had only to climb down the ladder, open the door, say briefly, 'It's *this* that matters, this act of love—not marriage or any other cockeyed manmade custom.' It was after all what he'd been preaching to her for years.

123

But he stayed where he was, believing he was dreaming as his mind strayed down long avenues of convention, confronting thoughts he would never even consider, save with derision, in waking moments : playing the game, treating one's woman with honour, avoiding licentiousness like the plague—the phrases hung in the corridors like grim-lipped stags' heads uttering Victorian warnings, they were the warnings out of which had grown the petty conventions he'd sneered at ever since he'd realised he had a mind of his own and could use it his own way.

Well, he was dreaming. Impossible to imagine he'd been awake and thinking nonsense like that. But he had to get away, out into the open air for a bit, it would be a good substitute for bromide.

Carefully he went down the ladder. It creaked and he knew Doris's pulse raced. He stood outside her door filling his pipe, shredding the tobacco carefully. He could hear voices—the voices of people whispering. He was certain they were whispering about him—*to* him, rather. These islanders—they were uninhibited, happiness had bred a disregard in them. But he had to remember he and Doris were going back. (He was off down the avenues again, the stags pursed their lips and the warnings echoed through the respectable corridors).

Gripping his pipe tightly between his teeth he went softly downstairs (fancifully, he imagined the voices pursuing, tempting him) and out into the summer night of stars.

He wasn't wrong about the voices, but whose they were he couldn't be sure—there were so many people now on the island. Once he thought he identified Brutus Robinson's . . . " walking round the island, leaving his girl to lie lonely " and a snatch of *Musensohn;* but he went on walking, his pipe firm in his teeth, his arms swinging determinedly.

It took him all night to walk to the top of the island and down again. By the time he returned weariness had drawn the edge off his desire. Robinson, catching fish in the river, saw him return. He returned himself to the inn with his three spread fish. " Such a fuss over not being married. If I'd known he was so particular I'd have married them myself."

" You," de Montfort said. He warmed beeswax in his hand and glanced sideways along the polished surface of the table. " I suppose you've a yarn tucked away somewhere about being an ordained priest."

" No yarn. I've got the announcement cut from *The Times* somewhere. ' Church appointments and ordinations.' That was in Leicester in—ah, I've forgotten the date. I was a curate, on the way to becoming a rural dean when I found the confines of the church too restricting. I took—"

There were footsteps on the stairs. " Here comes Harold Bassett, tidy in body and mind." De Montfort's eyelid closed heavily over his bright eye. " Brutus Robinson was just telling me that if he'd known what store you set by it he'd have married you. He's a priest—ordained, and with a paper to prove it."

Robinson thought with silent joy of this opportunity to watch Harold play wolf—innocently. " You can take my word for it," he said with unction.

" He's a man of action," de Montfort said, spreading the wax. " He'd marry you today and quench your thirst thereby."

" You mean you really—?" Harold departed joyfully upstairs again. Doubtless suspicion lurked somewhere in his mind but he gave it no countenance. " There's absolutely no reason why we shouldn't be married today—at noon," he said, having explained to Doris.

" Oh Hal. Oh Hal."

She was married in the cotton dress she had worn since the day of their arrival. " Getting dressed up's just a pagan symbol: none of the hocus-pocus matters: it's the signing of the register that does the trick "—his words, repeated in all their rendezvous from Harringay to the Corner House, came flooding back to both of them. They both flushed and ascribed their embarrassment to false reasons. Even Robinson was not dressed up: Loomes was a tall man; his cassock and surplice were too much of a tent for Robinson's taste. " There's no rules about priestly garb : I can marry you as well in dungarees as in glad rags. I remember an occasion in Leicester—" but his remembrance was pinched out by Janet Tiptree. " Enough: there's a limit to what even wishful thinkers will believe." Brutus Robinson went on down to Sumer Church, his face composed for the occasion. " If I've lied today—" Janet Tiptree hushed him again. " Call down no oaths. Leave them where they are and save your soul." He shrugged. " Belief or no belief, a fact is a fact."

The church held about a hundred and twenty. About twice that number squeezed themselves in. Outside there were crowds, since there was little distance for the news to travel. They were crowds neither curious nor boisterous. They had walked over merely to wish whoever might be getting married well. They kept on the move, not singing and not gaping either, but just spreading up the slopes and along the lanes with tranquil patience, hoping perhaps by their massed presence to will happiness on the couple for ever.

Harold, shepherding Doris out of the church, his fingers at her elbow, felt a remote stirring of need to speak in rhetorical phrases. ' In this lovely place of happy hours . . .' but he murmured no more than this. The crowds

126

moved back as he and Doris returned to *The Lute Player*.
" You know," he whispered with a trace of uneasiness,
" There's more people here than ever. It's . . ." but the
word ' frightening ' would not come. Doris took his hand.
" We're married. O Hal, it's wonderful ! But I can't sort
of believe it somehow."

" Silly," he said, bringing himself down to her level of
conversation without thinking or regretting.

Together they went into the room where the wine stood
on the table, purple in the sunlight, and the villagers stood
round to welcome them, the nudges and the joke about
Robinson playing priest suppressed now.

They all filled their glasses and drank. " Happiness !" It
was like the finale of a lavish musical comedy ; at the open
windows and doors people were crowding, and behind them
more people pressed forward. The word Happiness faded
back among them, a diminishing echo.

When all the wine was drunk and all the wishes spoken
it was dusk. De Montfort took down the lute from the wall
and Brutus Robinson sang a song he'd learned on the
island, a love song. Everyone sang with him and when the
song was ended Harold Bassett and Doris Cheesman had
gone from the room. There was a silence, then the sound
of a stair creaking, then laughter as de Montfort remarked
incredulously, " They're together at last."

The laughter sounded above, and as Doris unpacked the
peach satin nightie at last she thought, ' All my life I'll
remember that laughter, like an omen.' Somewhere in
recollection was a movie with a rose arbour and a creaking
gate which the hero would annually vow to oil and which
was still creaking plaintively as hero and heroine faded to
misty distance framed by the rose arbour and bidden to
eternal romance by an invisible angelic choir and throbbing
strings. It was the kind of recollection that came naturally

to her. Her eyes were bright with misty sentimental tears, and as she looked at Harold she saw that he too was hiccoughing a little with emotion.

Two days later they went over to see Loomes. He had recovered and was about again. " We must get you married. It's less than a week to your return, isn't it?"

Harold and Doris looked from the window. Their little fingers were linked. That morning they had walked along the eastern coast of the island and had seen three small ships stationary in the bay; and in the fields there were shacks, completed now and with people living in them— people who should have returned to England weeks before. The ships had steam up, their funnels breathed faintly, but they appeared to be anchored, and no-one could say why they were there.

" We're married," they said, springing their pleasant surprise.

Loomes buttoned his faded blue shirt. " Married. Ah. You must accept my good wishes. Married by whom, one wonders. A visitor in holy orders presumably?"

They told him, watching the laughter break on his face, listening with slight umbrage as its sound filled the room.

" What's so funny?" To calm himself Harold took out his pipe and filled it.

" Funny? I'm amused, my dear children, at your credulity—at the thought of Brutus Robinson playing parson— at your sophistication being overcome by his innocent yarning—"

Umbrage faded to the trumpets of shock. Their fingers unlinked themselves, were drawn away sharply as if from contagion. But Harold, flushing, could not bring himself to the admission of guilelessness. " Of course I suspected all along . . . I mean, no-one could believe anything he said . . . I mean, that yarn about the frog, and that other one about the time-keeping job . . ." Boldly he flung the gauntlet, shrugged: " What does it matter? The marriage business was just a gesture"

" Harold !"

" You're so strung up with conventions," he said. " I knew they'd haunt you all the time, that you'd spoil our life thinking it was lived in sin." With raised eyebrows and a smoke-ring, in control of umbrage and shock and everything else now, he added: " And now we are. There's nothing we can do about it." He had the comfortable feeling of having been operated on successfully without even being aware of the anaesthetic. " Unless Brutus Robinson really is a parson."

" It's most unlikely," Loomes said. " Like the rest of the jobs he tells you about. I know him fairly well." He was amused still—certainly not shocked, nor even reproving. " You must let me know what you want me to do."

" Yes," Doris said. She felt faint, indecent. Whatever Harold said you couldn't help feeling a bit like a . . . whore —she dragged the thought up determinedly. " We must think what to do." It seemed to her that if Loomes married them properly in a day or two everything might be—well, almost all right.

But in the end they did exactly nothing, because living in sin was after all a state they'd always flaunted flagrant approval of. And in a day or two it achieved a kind of coziness that, supported by the island happiness, was very pleasant indeed—as if the life they'd been secretly ashamed to aim at had suddenly been attained with no bother, no shame at all. " Because after all, it wasn't our fault. We didn't know." The pipe glowed and contented puffs were blown into the enchanted air of Happyland; and Doris felt delightfully, beautifully, wicked.

I

IX

FITCH and Mountalban were together again. "We're getting old." Fitch sidled in on his rubber soles. "We need each other's company."

He sat down and flicked the desk-lamp's funnel of light away from him. There was a certain pleasure to be gained by probing deep into failure when the failure was not his. Fitch hadn't the capacity for cynicism, but a little gloating always did him good. "Your idea of setting a guard of ships around Happyland hasn't been altogether successful." His tone bore a gloss of sympathy. "Not that it's your fault if people dodge the ships as easily as they dodge taxes. Of course your orders are being carried out : constant look-outs in the crows'-nests by day, searchlight sweeping the water by night. But people always find a way to get what they want. And they want happiness as they've never wanted anything before." He tipped his fingers together. "Well, of course that was your aim. You can't altogether blame them."

Mountalban accepted the jeer like a burden. He allowed Fitch minor pleasures. "Have you anything for me, Mr. Fitch?"

"I was at Cradle's this morning. There were only the Minister and old Drew there. And the staff of course. Lots of places are looking empty nowadays. Drew was lost— lost : he had no-one to introduce. He said to the Minister, 'You know, Minister, I don't know why you and I don't go to this place, this Happyland.' And the Minister said in that unctuous tone of his, 'Naturally the House—indeed all responsible persons—feel it their duty to make sacrifices in the national interest.' And later on he dropped a word, just a word, about the Honours List. I thought I caught a name—Baron Prospect of Elysium."

"Yes," Mountalban said. His resentment was never obviously bitter, but it was there—he wore it like a wrinkled lining to the dark clerkly clothes. "One knows of course that his organisation of disorganisation must have government backing. Of course the Minister's had to—er—accept a lot of blame for losing Happyland in the first place."

"The Minister's a dolt."

"It rankles with him, that knowledge. He's full of glee now. O yes, doubtless full of glee, Mr. Fitch." Mountalban opened a folder in which the news agencies' summaries had been made for him. 'Happyland Crisis looms Near.' It's all there—even accusation."

"Accusation?"

"The enormous financial gains. 'It is of course greatly to Mr. Mountalban's advantage to pack the island with as many people as possible.'"

"And isn't it?"

"The organisation for collecting money from those who stopped on broke down weeks ago. How, in a spellbound place, could it do otherwise? Of course I sent officers over. They too have not returned. Are you surprised, Mr. Fitch? And now, with a guard of ships round the place, people are still getting in—swimming, chartering aircraft, parachuting down. They go, not because they believe, but because greed and lust and curiosity and the self-hypnotised mania for something new have possessed them. And that same greed and lust and mania moves in those who are left behind, who have not yet discovered a way of getting to the island. So they make of themselves the wronged faction, denied their bomb, denied their happiness, denied everything but the power of numbers." He tapped his finger on the teletyped reports. "It's all there, between the lines."

Fitch polished his spectacles. "In my pocket there's an evening paper. It adds something, a comment perhaps." He unfolded the paper carefully, adjusted the desk-lamp. "An advertisement for a correspondence course in Happiness. 'Be independent of commercial undertakings,' it says; 'acquire your Happiness at home in easy stages. No apparatus.' You see, you really have done something big. One can go nowhere without being aware of it."

Again Mountalban tapped the folder. "A petition, organised by a Mr. Cheesman of Tooting Bec. 'Mr. Cheesman expects to get two million signatures to his We Want Our Happiness petition. He is to present it to Parliament next week. "Since we lost our Doris," Mr. Cheesman said in an interview, "there's been nothing in our lives. We think we're entitled to a bit of Happiness."' And I too am entitled to my happiness, Mr. Fitch."

But it had come to mean something different. His spiritual gropings were for the simple, the sincere. Too late he saw that to elude the magnitude of commerce was beyond him. With secret shame he thought of the inner satisfaction he had felt as time and time again he had woven the strands of business. He looked back over a life of success. He had failed in nothing. Clinging to success he raised his eyes to Fitch's eyes. "Things take possession, Mr. Fitch, they have a way of eluding control——"

There was a knock at the door. The first secretary entered. "The Minister."

Fitch departed silently and the Minister entered. Pomp and circumstance gave him their own particular hallowing and he glanced expectantly round the room before speaking, as if waiting for trumpets. In lieu of trumpets he blew out his own cheeks. " Things are taking a serious turn." He had the look of a debased cherub. For a moment the portrait of the three-months-old child on the silk cushion in the high-class photographer's studio showed through. His brain had remained static since then, his uselessness was etched round his thin lips, his hands were the thieving filthy hands of the inky schoolboy who had proudly and with due pomp returned on foundation day forty years later to utter soothing fatuities about his own lack of prowess. " Yes : a serious turn."

Mountalban laid his hands on the deck. His spatted feet were neatly together, his personality was enclosed somewhere invisible in a chrysalis of mediocrity. He too proclaimed his uselessness in a way, but there was too a shadow of humility. One expected him to say with an edge of self-pity, ' I've done my best. No man can do more.' What he actually said was, " A glass of sherry?"

Sipping the sherry the Minister exhibited mollification : it was a gambit; with his experience as a man of the world —he prided himself—he knew just what to do. " You know, my dear Mountalban, numbers are a very strange thing. They're so inconceivable. Look down from the roof of this building and you'll see London teeming. Yet there are three hundred thousand vanished from the land "— he spread his hand with careful effect—" vanished. And every day my colleague in Labour keeps me informed. Shipyards, mining, steel, food distribution—all are losing workers quicker than they can be kept track of. And there is no cessation—no cessation at all. People just draw out their savings—sometimes they don't even bother to do that—gather their families together and go—vanish. And where do they vanish to? Where, my dear Mountalban?"

Mountalban said nothing. The Minister must have his little histrionic fling.

" Of course to Happyland. It's serious, very serious. A two-hundredth part of the entire population : it may not sound very many, but you can take my word for it that the P.M. views the matter with the utmost gravity. Yes. The very utmost gravity. For there is no cessation, no cessation at all—only a steady, a constant, drain on the people of this . . . this land of ours. They have gone berserk. In pursuit of happiness they are sacrificing the very life-blood of their country." The Minister stood with his sherry gleaming, his hand nicely placed on his hip, his tongue delicately poised for a new phrase. " And unless something is done—"

" Have you any particular suggestion, Mr. Minister?" Mountalban's voice was smooth, almost disinterested.

" Naturally, my dear Mountalban—naturally. That is what I've come for. It isn't customary for a Minister of the Crown to waste time—his own or anyone else's."

" Well?" This time the word snapped out. The Minister started. A little of the sherry spilt. He sat down, easing his trousers deliberately over his knees. He needed a moment to regain breath, confidence. " His Majsty's Government are intending to vote a further two hundred million for nuclear research—insofar as that science is concerned with defence. Now, my dear Mountalban—" From the pocket of his embroidered waistcoat the Minister took a slip of paper. " Gideon Mills Corporation, Electrical Enterprises, Findlater's Chemical Development Corporation, Heavy Industries Limited—I think I'm right in saying you hold a controlling interest in all of them? Yes? Of course there's hardly a financial pie in Europe that hasn't a Mountalban finger in it—eh? Perhaps one might even say in the world. Amazing to me. I was always a complete duffer at school. Always. Only last week when I gave the foundation-day address I amused the boys by—but I mustn't digress." He looked across the desk and into the mild incurious eyes, at the neat collar and grey foulard tie, thinking ' Insipid little horror. Reminds me of Drew—neutral, petty, no sex, no character. Probably wears a nightshirt and drinks malted milk at bedtime.'

Carefully Mountalban said : " Don't hurry yourself on my account." He always let people say what they had to say. There was so much advantage to be gained from listening rather than talking, he'd learnt that from Fitch.

" Well, of course, sub-contracts would amount to—er—shall we say a hundred and fifty millions. Your shareholders—I happen to be one of them myself, in a very small way of course—would approve very strongly, I feel sure."

Impassively Mountalban rose and poured another sherry for the Minister. " So?"

" So if only this wretched business of Happyland could be cleaned up we could go ahead with our nuclear fission experiments, confident in the knowledge that there would be no further draining away of the populace at a critical time."

The tape machine ticked suddenly. Neither of the two men paid any attention. After a moment the ticking ceased. " All times are critical, are they not, Mr. Minister?"

" In a sense, I suppose." Sherry tingled on the Minister's tongue; the wine was like a switch to his rhetoric. " But with communism staining half the world with its red blood—"

" I never understood politics," Mountalban said. It was true. " I understand money. Happyland has been a very serious loss to me. With the good intentions of an—an apostle of the simple life I deliberately arranged for the very minimum of form-filling and bureaucracy. People get so tired of it, you know. They paid their money in advance and their accommodation was arranged. Naturally they were encouraged to stay longer. That too was all arranged —one of our guides collected payments and forwarded the remittances by the returning ships or aircraft. But when everybody stayed and to them was added a constant influx, most of them on forged warrants bought on the black market—"

The Minister nodded sympathetically. " I know. We've got the Special Branch looking into that."

" —of course things got out of hand. The Special Branch?" Mountalban spoke entirely without irony. " One hopes they're investigating the next honours list."

The Minister ignored this. " So you'd expect to be compensated not only for the price of the island but for your losses too?"

" As I said, I understand money." Shame pricked, but his tone was the tone of a floorwalker explaining the reasons for his humble request for an increase in salary. " You, Mr. Minister, being a shareholder, no doubt understand it too."

The monocle flicked and the Minister rose, hand on hip, fingers down-pointing on his firm buttock. " The basic principles, I suppose." Pausing, he added, " Happyland would then become state property. It would be used, of course, for the benefit of the nation; that is to say in its defence. One must do what is best for the nation as a whole. One can't have the lifeblood, the people, slowly draining away, seeking happiness. The position would be impossible—intolerable. I saw danger there long ago. The red light. I told the P.M.—"

Mountalban listened gently to what the Minister told the P.M. When the Minister had gone he summoned Fitch. " The government wants to buy Happyland from me and reimburse me for my losses into the bargain."

"A business triumph, I take it. A *volte face* of the world of commerce—eh?"

Yes, it was a triumph—but it soured in Mountalban's comprehension. "It wasn't what I wanted, Mr. Fitch." From somewhere he evoked the dead desire to see people happy. "I wanted to fulfil the Happyland story, to do everything that vulgarian Creech said I could do—inaugurate a pilgrimage. It would have been something, surely it would have been *something*, to offer them—"

Finger alongside his nose Fitch said: "Perhaps you offered it a little too eagerly. You forgot the ease with—ah—which they can be persuaded to believe. You also forgot their greed. Ah yes, they're a greedy lot, people." He ran his hand gently to and fro across his chest, waiting for the heartburn to subside. "Each man destroys the thing he loves: it's an old saying, very true."

Softly Mountalban said: "Truth is something that foxes me, Mr. Fitch. The half-truth—I have been familiar with that all my life. That is why Creech and I were able to return from Happyland: because we never really believed. And those who do return—they are in the same case, they are the cynics who recognise that they've been believing because they were told to believe. But there are too few of them. It's the others we're concerned with, the ones who, impelled by greed or lust or mere curiosity, are invading the island and are finding that that which I scarcely believed myself, Mr. Fitch, is true. One would have thought that there were more cynics and fewer simpletons. But it seems not." He rose and went to the tape machine. "'Happyland Crisis. It is estimated that the number of people on Happyland now exceeds half a million.' The Minister's figures were a little dated."

In the streets the placards fluttered: *Special Cabinet*

Meeting, and on the radio news at nine o'clock came the announcement of the taking over of Happyland by the government. Mountalban presided at a board meeting the following day. " It's the government's responsibility now, gentlemen."

Narrowing his eyes against the cigar smoke he observed that it was recognised that he had made an astute move. " In exchange for the Happyland enterprise, which we have proved an impracticable asset, we receive orders which will greatly enrich some of our other enterprises. We also recoup our losses on the Happyland scheme. I take it you're satisfied, gentlemen?"

He drove through London in his ancient sedate limousine during the afternoon. *News of Happyland.* One always made a good profit from one's newspapers in times when the public's pulse beat fast. But naturally there was nothing in the papers he didn't know. Humourlessly he turned to the cartoon : he never understood them, his childish puzzlement was a secret shame : he laughed dutifully even when he was alone. Sogg had drawn a picture of the airway route to Happyland, the streamered balloons being shot at by ministerially-dressed men with popguns. ' Signs of the times '—he repeated the caption over to himself, but it made no sense.

He watched people at street corners buying newspapers, wondering what the government were going to do. He fought to create wonder in himself, but it was dead. He knew quite well what the government were going to do. His mind embraced *The Sorrows of Satan.* ' I am Judas,' he thought : ' I have betrayed.' But the sense of treachery was dead too.

In Trafalgar Square someone had tied a banner to the Column : " We want —" the words flapped away and above the banner the pigeons whirled. The Happyland sign on Grand Buildings was out—someone had given instructions. In Coventry Street the paintings of Bluecopse and Sumer had been taken away and the Happyland Quiz in the amusement arcade was marked *Out of Order*.

Outside the Mountalban Building a policeman moved people on. They tended to gather, not yet with sullen resentment but with the mild indifferent curiosity of sheep. "Move along there. You can't do anything. It's all in the government's hands now."

In the annexe of the beautiful room the Minister awaited him. "Half an hour," he said peevishly.

"I've been driving through London." He sat quietly at the walnut desk and a secretary came. "I very deeply regret that it has not been possible to achieve my original plan of offering Happiness on a commercial basis. As must be realised, my failure has largely been caused by the lack of coöperation of the public. Now that the government have taken over the island to avoid a crisis which would have ruined the nation I appeal to everyone on Happyland to follow whatever instructions are issued, for the good of us all." His voice was level, toneless. The secretary stood waiting. "Prepare that statement and circulate it to the press."

The Minister rocked on his heels. "We anticipate a bit of difficulty, getting people back again. Without threats, of course. And threats are—ah—unconstitutional. But we're going to try with the navy first. The good old navy, eh?"

"Just as a beginning," Mountalban said, thinking of the dead wonder, treachery distorted by incalculable traffickings of commerce, glimpsing for an instant the world's dilemma.

X

"CORRUPTION," the Captain said. "That's what at the bottom of it all." He was the bulldog breed: his cabin was spartan in the extreme. He had neither wife nor family and he was bitterly proud of his solitude. This cabin with its rigid bed and grey blank walls betokened his asceticism. "What do you say, Mr. Forsyth?"

"Almost certainly, sir." The young officer stood rigidly to attention. In the wardroom it was permissible to relax sufficiently to smile at the proper kind of humour—the kind that belittled people who didn't understand the navy's glory; but elsewhere not at all. "The Minister's come aboard, sir."

The Captain saw the Minister in his cabin. There was only one chair and the Minister sat in it—by the Captain's orders, one might have said.

"This is the ultimatum, so to speak." The Minister's small uneven teeth parted with wan humour as he handed the thick envelope over. "Their Lordships, of course, have given you their orders?"

The Captain's thumb lightly touched the embossed red seals. His orders were to catapult the document over in an aircraft, then organise the evacuation of the island.

He now took the Minister up on the bridge. The island lay to port in a misty nimbus of midday heat. "Look through there."

The Minister bent carefully and put his eye to the glass. With his monocle dangling and his homburg held on his hand he had all the furtive insouciance of a middle-aged solicitor enjoying a peepshow on Southend pier.

The island flattened itself against the end of the glass like a graven scene on a medallion. There was a field bounded by flower-starred hedgerows and among the scantily-built shelters people appeared for a moment enchanted in attitudes of pent movement. It was like one of those scenes depicted on the coinage and banknotes of republics that wrest glory from the good earth. The scythe and the plough and all the symbols of good husbandry were there, and the women, patient and enduring, with their blond children running in the sunlight.

"By George!" the Minister said; "there's a hell of a lot of 'em. Thank God we took the right action at the right time. Place would have been ridden with pest and starvation before long. You can see that a mile off."

When he stood up from the glass the detail vanished and the land lay softened by mist, still and silent. But in spite of the stillness, the silence, the island conveyed somehow across the water the fact that it was alive. There was the awareness of countless numbers waiting, not in arms or even with any attempt to resist anything that might happen, but rather as if with passive assurance they knew they were bound to triumph in the end. As if their happiness were the end of it all—unanswerable, inviolable, supreme.

The Minister took the handkerchief from his cuff and touched his lips with it. "I don't like it: to be honest I don't like it." The sun gleamed on his oiled hair, his fear, his dim autocracy. "They're moving about there working *et cetera,* as if nothing at all troubled them. Yet they must be aware we're here, they must wonder about us." There was a self-pitying reproach in his tone, his petulance was that of a child, and the Captain sardonically imagined him stamping his feet. "They must wonder—they must—"

There had in fact been wonder on the island, but it

was a wonder that could wait. There was all the time in the world. One of the effects of happiness was a release from the tyranny of time. It was as if the present moment were prolonged indefinitely. Somewhere in the mind the day of return, with its datal number, its hour of departure and its long antagonism to the ecstasy of peace, had a kind of inevitable existence, symbolised by the printed slip that reposed forgotten in countless handbags and waistcoat pockets: *The Day and Hour of your Return to England is ....p.m. on the......... Please be at the quay with all your baggage at least* 30 *minutes before this time to allow for necessary checking and documentation*. But it was an existence as remote for most people as the day of judgment. The prolonged moment of happiness was enough. So when several weeks had elapsed and the ships in the bay suddenly multiplied to a chain that encircled the whole island there was the same curiosity that might have arisen over the sudden manifestation of an unseasonable storm; no more than that. It was not that the new populace could imagine no reason for the ships' presence—from time to time in the crowded village streets and besieged fields an acknowledgement of their ultimate purpose could be inferred from the ripple of apprehension that would run flamewise among a group, a crowd, a multitude—but rather that the disaster they foretold lay outside the extended moment's happiness, beyond care, beyond the unassailable perfection of the island's enchantment.

" They're a good way out," Harold Bassett said. He stood with Doris on the crest of the hill that hid river and vineyard and the ceaseless movements of people whose songs and speech rose faintly up, tattered by distance. There was no longer any solitude on the island, but the sense of solitude had not been destroyed: every person possessed it individually, it was the same solitude that descends on a crowd when an announcement of death or calamity is made, yet here it was brought about by happiness.

Two of the villagers passing on their way to work in the fields called greetings. " Mr. and *Mrs.* Bassett." They kept straight faces, there was no innuendo in their manner, yet they contrived to point the joke. Doris flushed; the hereditary shame had not yet been overcome. Maybe three months was too short a time to drive it out. " They don't have any need to draw attention—"

" Ah, sanfairyan." Harold's shame was glossed with a tricky amusement, a defiant contempt. They'd never get married now. The situation appealed. Dimly in recollection the shocked neighbours stood, whispers rioted in the suburbs. They'd be appalled beyond measure, there would be delight in a nose-thumbing defiance. " If we ever get back we'll show 'em just how much we don't care."

" If . . ."

Later that day down on the western shore they saw some more people landing—a family of four, parents and a boy and a girl. The boy carried in his arms a copper-eyed striped cat. They came ashore from a small motorboat. The father stepped onto the sand and drew from his pocket a note case and counted fifty notes, carefully. He wore a neat bowler and a grey suit. He handed the boatman the money. Immediately the boat turned and skimmed off through the surf. The family watched it out to sea. They stood with their hands shading their eyes, all in precisely the same attitude, rigid and immaculate, until the white feather of spray was lost to sight. " He'll get challenged again," the man said. He turned to Harold and Doris. " We were challenged on the way out. One of those destroyer things sent a boat with a couple of sailors in it. ' Orders to let no-one past,' he said. But we'd been primed. We knew the way." With heavy solemnity he winked. "There's always a way." Whispering man-to-man he added, "After all, Christ was sold for thirty pieces of silver—that's three-pound-fifteen, even if you count it in half-crowns. I reckon we'll be about the last to make it, though. They've got a proper cordon round now. Everyone's being turned back. It's the government: they've taken over the island."

Harold jerked his pipe upward. "Parachute—that's the method that seems favoured now. They tell me it's very dear, though."

The man gathered his family to him. "O it wasn't the expense. We sold the house and the car and everything. But the wife won't let her feet go off the ground—will you, dear? Acrophobia. It's a distressing complaint, even stairs make her come over funny sometimes. But we're here now. 'To hell with the government and the country and everything else,' we said. 'We're entitled to what there is on the face of the earth.' So we sold up everything just like that and came." For a moment anxiety clouded his eyes: he wore anxiety like a familiar suit. "It's . . . I mean . . . we haven't wasted our—"

"Sit down and rest," Doris said. "You'll see."

They sat down on the warm sand. "Food," the woman said. "That's what bothers me. The papers in England said Mountalban's stocks were running out."

"They are; but nobody cared for them much—tinned sardines, condensed milk, tinned sausages. There's land. You can grow things on it; and there are rivers full of fish and cows full of milk and chickens full of eggs. We eat the rabbits too. It stops them ruining the crops."

"But with so many people here—?"

"There's enough."

It was true. So far there had been enough. In a happy place people bother singularly little about food.

144

Loomes and de Montfort and Janet Tiptree had formed themselves into a committee. It couldn't be called a government, since the island had never needed a government and the increase of its population, all of whom achieved happiness, a state that needs neither protection nor control, made no difference to the conditions obtaining. But the seat of it, whatever it was, was at *The Lute Player*. There the three of them would answer questions put to them by the leaders of other committees representing various groups of the island's old and new population. They were mostly simple questions about the location of places that needed workers and they were easily answered. Dairies, vineyards and farms had everyone they needed to extend their productiveness. The fallow land was ploughed and sown, the vineyard presses were increased in number, flower cultivation was diminished and flax and wheat extended. In the villages that wove cloth more looms were made and where a dozen women had sat a hundred now passed their shuttles to and fro. From the quarries men brought stone and built new villages almost overnight. The woods were thinned and the timber used for houses and the simplest kind of furniture. But nowhere was beauty desecrated. Since everyone had an essential interest in the place spoliation was of no advantage to anyone.

The first question the committee had been faced with was the problem of money. But as there was no longer any possibility of trade with England money was found to be unnecessary and quickly abandoned. " Some time in the future," Loomes said, " we'll notice our deficiency in metal. There are tin and copper in the island but no iron. So we shall either have to resume trade with England or contrive substitutes. It may be that when the hubbub and the shouting have died down over there we may be able to barter our tin and copper for their iron and steel, in such small quantities as we need, without a resumption of the use of money."

It, and similar problems, were of the future; and because happiness is a thing of the present they were let be.

One day Harold Bassett had shaken their return ticket from his pocket. The date on it had long passed. " We were not at the quay with our baggage thirty minutes before the time of departure." He tried to make a joke of it, but the need to make that kind of joke had gone. But the mention of the ticket had served its purpose : without making any overt decision it was now plain to each of them that they would stay. " I'd feel ever so awkward, going back now, not married . . ." vaguely Doris sought for reasons. " It seems all right here somehow now that time's gone by a bit, but back home . . . I don't know." She puckered her brow, recalling Tooting Bec; but it would not be recalled.

So they stayed on. Like everyone else with a veneer of sophistication glossing an inherent simplicity they were easily spellbound. They found work on the land easy and satisfying. " It'll last us a lifetime." There was neither need nor desire to return to the other world.

Then one morning they saw the aircraft catapulted from the deck of one of the ships. It hovered over the island. It was high enough for everyone on the island to see it. Faces were upturned and from the plane it must have appeared to the crew that all over the island there was a sudden blooming of eyes, as if the fragments of glass in a kaleidoscope had shifted into a new pattern.

The small container fell with incredible slowness across the sky and the plane had crossed the island and turned before the parachute opened and drifted. Everywhere people ran, anticipating its direction, and when it eventually landed in the wild garden of the manse the noise of their massing had its own strange quality of apprehension, as the hideous sweating silence of soldiers entering a mined village tells of their fear.

In the garden the parachute strung itself limply over the branches of a pear tree. Some of the fruit jerked to the ground with small thuds. The black metal container swung for a moment, thumping against the trunk. In the branches above the yellow silk glimmered and subsided like a pricked blister.

The crowds had entered the garden, but they came carefully, backed by numbers that stretched in seething movement up and down the slopes. From all over the island people were hurrying, as if the wave of apprehension had been airborne across the length and breadth of Happyland. Their gathering was like a flower uncurling more and more of the edges of its immense petals; and at its centre was the orchard of the manse, its heavy lush grass, its burdened tree, the black container diminishing its thuds now as it hung there on silk cords.

Loomes moved forward with de Montfort and Janet Tiptree. From the edge of the orchard countless eyes watched them.

" Something they've got to say to us," Loomes said. He unscrewed the container and took the sealed envelope and held it high. " ' To Whom it may Concern.' "

The seals broke and dropped their dry dust like bloodspots among the grass, and Loomes took out the single sheet of heavy foolscap embossed with the arms of England and sealed with the Prime Minister's seal and his neat firm inflexible signature.

" To everyone on the island known generally as Happyland, the piece of land whose geographical position is determined by the figures of Latitude and Longitude herebelow given:

147

" Take notice that, in consequence of the ignoring of repeated warnings by His Majesty's Government that any mass migration to Happyland would dislocate the industries of the country to which its natives are in honour bound, and by statute impelled, to remain faithful so long as they shall live, His Majesty's Government have now decided on a course of action, viz:

" His Majesty's Government have purchased from its private owner the island of Happyland. The island is to be used as a target in the trial of the new X-bomb in the very near future. His Majesty's Government have reluctantly come to the conclusion that in face of world unrest they would be failing in their duty if they did not take adequate measures for the defence of the population against all possible aggression. Since the claim of the physicists concerned is that the X-bomb will completely obliterate from the globe all trace of the land on which it falls it is considered essential that immediate proof of its efficacy be forthcoming, so that potential aggressors may be made aware of our strength. It is scarcely necessary to add that His Majesty's Government and His Majesty's Allies have no intention of using the X-bomb as a weapon of unprovoked attack.

" It has not been possible to find any other suitable target for the X-bomb. At the same time the advice of His Majesty's experts gathered together to form a Royal Commission is that any continuation of mass migration to Happyland on a scale similar to that which has taken place in the last few months would be bound to lead to starvation, disease, and an extensive death-toll. The members of the Royal Commission are of the opinion that the island of Happyland is too

148

small to support even its present excessive population without long-term building plans and industrialisation on a scale that cannot be contemplated in the present state of world unrest. Therefore, apart from the need for Happyland as a bomb target, it has inevitably become necessary to evacuate the island to ensure the safety of the misguided thousands who have invaded it without any regard for the rights of its late owner or for the principles of commerce.

"Evacuation will commence at dawn following the delivery of this ultimatum. As leader of His Majesty's Government I feel sure that I can count now on the wholehearted coöperation of everyone concerned without the necessity of taking additional strenuous measures.

"The ships of the Royal Navy that now surround the island will move as close inshore as possible. Organisation of the embarking parties will be left entirely under your control, but it is hoped that every effort will be made to complete the evacuation with the utmost expedition."

Loomes' voice ceased. He looked toward the crowds who watched. He had spoken slowly and deliberately, not raising his voice above the level he used for his sermons in church. There was no need to do so. Those on the inmost edge of the crowd could hear him perfectly well. They stood while he was reading, men women and children alike, in attitudes of serenity. They were attentive, silent, but no more than that. With the reading of each successive paragraph no response of fear or resentment—or for that matter of pleasure either—manifested itself. And although the words could not have carried beyond the depth of a hundred or so people at this inmost fringe of the vast crowd, and although all the time people were arriving and adding

149

their number to the slowly unfurling outer edges, so that even when the ultimatum was read the crowd was still only a third as big as it was to become as people, magnetised by news, came hurrying from whatever had occupied them —even so there was silence, so that when Loomes ceased speaking and took from somewhere about him a pin and walked from the orchard onto the road and along the road a little way to where a magnolia stood at the edge and pinned the document to the trunk, the small taps of the stone on the pin were clearly audible.

All the rest of that day people filed past the notice, reading it—or reading as much as was necessary to confirm those of its clauses they had heard of so far only by rumour—and passing on, still without showing fear or resentment. Then they began to gather in small groups all over the island. Loomes and de Montfort and Janet Tiptree returned to *The Lute Player*. There too a group had gathered and were talking. It wasn't so much that a course of action was being decided as that it had become clear to everyone that, because they were happy, only one course lay open.

Night came and still the groups of people were gathered. Their voices could be heard everywhere in the darkness, but nightingales sang on unrestrained. Then, although no tumult had arisen, no argument taken place, it seemed as if all over the island people had reached the same decision independent of each other. Again the quiet urgent ceaseless movement began; and again, as in the afternoon, everyone drifted to his appointed place without the orders of any leader.

And when that was done it was dawn.

XI

A T 04.00 hours the order was given and the boats were lowered. All round the island ships had moved inshore and the tackle hung limply from davits on cleared decks. " No coddling," the Captain had snapped during his briefing. " They're not travellers, they're not personnel, they're just people. Crowd 'em—in the holds, on the decks, anywhere so long as the ships' efficiency isn't impaired. I want to get the lot in one go. Their Lordships have got us buggering about here on a school treat. That's what it is, gentlemen : a bloody school treat. And the sooner it's over the better."

The armada of boats closed in on the island. Overhead an observation plane from the aircraft carrier hung with whirring wings. The pilot watched the boats moving inward like a tightening noose. The haze of a new day's heat gathered in the valleys and from it the hills rose miraculously bright with the sheen of dew. The pilot dropped to five hundred feet. From there he could plainly see people moving unhurriedly from inland toward the sea. He climbed and crossed the island and descended again. The same movement. The pilot called the flight-deck of his ship. " They're moving all right, they're making a sort of chain round the island, they're just about at the edge now, all round."

" All right. Boat commanders can group them. I suppose they've got piles of pestering luggage?"

The pilot went down to two-fifty feet. From there he could see the people's faces upturned, watching him, could see the children pointing. " No luggage visible," he reported. He cruised around, crossed the island again.

Every village was deserted. He could see the dust on the streets, scuffed as by a pilgrimage to a spot beside an orchard where the remains of yesterday's parachute hung on a tree. Even the morning fires had been lit, and around the bivouac shelters of the newer settlers he glimpsed garments laid flat on the grass to dry. It was all as if everyone meant to return in an hour or so. He was puzzled, but it wasn't his duty to be puzzled. His job was to report what he saw. He reported it.

"O?" the flight-deck said. "You mean it looks like trouble?"

"I wouldn't know," the pilot said. He had a fresh young face and a floozie in a pub in Guildford. He kept up the dated slang for her sake. "But it certainly doesn't look as if they've packed up ready to go."

"Then what the hell are they on the shore for?"

"I wouldn't know that either," the pilot said.

The boat commanders had their orders: no member of the crews was to step ashore; nor were the boats to be beached. "Make 'em wade out," the Captain had said. The strategy was to hold the boats in shallow water, load them to capacity ("But not a man, woman or child more." The Captain hated the job, but standing orders would be obeyed to the letter; even vindictiveness wouldn't sway him) and return to their ships immediately. There was no certain knowledge of the exact number of people on the island, but it was thought that they could all be accommodated on the ships. The boats would have to make relay journeys until everyone was taken off.

Day had broken now. Sunlight flecked the steel-surfaced water; spatters of yellow broken and glinting and feathered with wakes as the boats converegd on the island.

The island, viewed in whole by the thousand eyes of the boats' crews, was somehow—perhaps by the association of ideas and accepted beliefs, by the insistent dogma of commerce—evocative of happiness. It wasn't the faintly exotic beauty, the serenity, or in any way the physical aspect of the land; at least, not alone. There was apparently a spirit investing the place; and as if in bemused antipathy it infused the air invisibly like perfume, or ghosts, or the echo of recent laughter. The island seemed to be not only waiting but watching too.

And as the first boats anchored and the crews ceased rowing and turned their eyes toward the island they saw that they were indeed being watched.

All round the island the people had gathered on the shore. They had set themselves on sand and beach and rock and pasture, had made of themselves a human chain encircling the island. They stood, some of them separated only by a yard or so, so that it appeared that they were disposed for some vast round game and that they only awaited a signal to join hands and dance.

But they remained still; and their stillness, their passivity, was impressive in a way that no action, no sound, could have been impressive. They simply stood there and looked toward the boats that were now shipping oars and anchoring all round the island.

There was no aggression in their manner, nor for that matter any acceptance either. It was simply the expression of mute inviolability; as if without need for either speech or message they conveyed their rejection of the ultimatum.

They could feel as they stood there the happiness of the island possessing them, and this too was conveyed in their stance and manner. It was as if, finding the necessity to reject the ultimatum, they had been fortified during the night by the very knowledge of the boundlessness of the happiness that existed there but which till now they had drawn on only in tiny measure.

It was a fortification extremely puzzling to the boat crews; and because it was strange it was strong.

So now for a time they faced each other: the happy and the hopeless, across the thin clear water and the coast of sand and rock and pasture, astonishment and a little fear in the eyes of the sailors, the heated words of normal life useless and unspoken on their tongues, their throats suddenly dry with the effort of putting into words their sense of failure; and in the eyes of those who watched from the shore the keen cool searching gaze that was neither arrogance nor pleading, since both those qualities formed no part of happiness, but was simply a statement of fact more factual than any words or action could have been: We will not return.

In one of the boats the sailors looked at each other. "That's that then." But it wasn't of course. Not yet—for they had their orders, and their orders were concrete, they had appeared in black and white, they had been handed down from officers to petty officers, from petty officers to crew. And they at least were tangible, they could be comprehended by the mind.

"Come on," one ordinary seaman said. He began to climb over the side of the boat. His foot was already touching the water when the P.O. commanding that particular boat said, "Get back. Weren't you told a dozen times? Isn't an order good enough for you?"

The ordinary seaman paused with his leg still over the side, his life-jacket adding a look of fantasy to his umbrage. His hands gripped the gunwale. They were thin calloused hands with triangular nails, and he lifted them suddenly in a gesture of dissociation. "Well, if you think you'll get that lot to come just by oglin' 'em—"

For a moment then no-one moved at all, neither in the boats nor on the shore. It was like being up against an unscalable wall. The boats rocked slightly and the sea imprinted its ceaseless patterns on the shore. The gulf between the happy people and those who had come to rescue them from happiness was perhaps two hundred yards. It might have been a thousand light years.

Then suddenly the sailors felt their impotence. They felt full of shame and did the only thing that occurred to them. In one boat the crew began to shout and gesticulate with enormous violence and in a moment the cries had been taken up from boat to boat. They began to assail the people on the island with small impotent angry gestures and with loud threatening cries. They asserted their voices and the sound grew to be a tumult—the thin bitter rage of men who did not understand and could only fall back on the passionate anger of children. It was a great indiscriminate sound and it carried across to the island and echoed round the hills and returned thinly across the water.

But it had no effect at all. The people on the island remained passive and still, continuing to show neither resentment nor acceptance but only the same stolid inviolable refusal.

After a while it became clear even to the sailors that those on the island would remain unvanquished, that there was nothing whatever to be done. In one of the boats one of the sailors fell suddenly silent in the midst of the shouting. Afterward his comrades recalled hearing him make a remark: he said with sudden relinquishment, " Whatever it is, if they believe in it that much it must be worth having." His eyes were bright with revelation, and afterward his mates were to recall that too, and his valediction as he jumped over the side and began to swim toward the shore and then to emerge, treading water, and walk slowly up the beach toward the waiting islanders until he stood among them and turned and formed one of their number :

"Sod the government and the navy too and every twerp without enough common sense to know a good thing when he sees it." Just the single obscenity remained, and the treachery, and their anger because he had been one of them and was now one against them.

"A bloody court-martial," the P.O. said with hopeless anger. "That's what the stupid ape gets when he gets back." But somehow they all knew it wasn't true, that it could never be true, that somewhere in their anger there was something fundamentally wrong.

But now in the moment of the traitor's sudden desertion his colleagues, seeing him dive, were suddenly silent; and as if the silence were like a thread drawing them together all the other crews fell silent too; and in five minutes there was no sound at all but the gentle ironical lapping of the sea against the boats. And although no order had been given the crews dipped their oars and in a few more moments, synchronised by the flag signals from their mother ships (the order was at last given to return) the whole armada began to move out again, to leave the island as quietly and as efficiently, and in the same precise pattern, but expanding now instead of contracting, as they had approached it.

The pilot of the observation plane had reported, "They're going back inland, getting on with their jobs. All over the island they're returning to work." His voice was excited, youthful.

"You're not doing a B.B.C. commentary," the flight-deck said with vindictive asperity. "All right. Return to base."

The pilot returned to his flight deck. "I'd've liked to touch down on that little berg," he mused.

Later that day, and for many days, the action off Happyland, and its failure, became public knowledge.

For three hours this morning the entire detailed fleet stood by round the coast of Happyland. Each ship had sent its entire complement of lifeboats to evacuate the island in accordance with the Government ultimatum. The Government's design was defeated by the massed passive resistance of the island's population. A special cabinet meeting is being called to consider the next step. A Government spokesman told this newspaper that the difficulties are enormously increased by the knowledge that the Happiness Spell might well affect 90 per cent of any naval personnel sent ashore to reason with the population. " But we shall never contemplate the use of force," he added.

That was only the beginning.

The case of Ordinary Seaman Yelland of Wookey Hole, who, in defiance of orders, went ashore during last week's disastrous attempt to evacuate Happyland is taking up too much of the Attorney-General's time and consideration. The case is a simple one. Yelland must be court-martialled on his return to this country. The problem that should be occupying the brains of the Attorney-General and all other authoritative persons is the problem of the evacuation of Happyland. We say fearlessly, here and now, that no plan should be refused consideration, even the most dire. After all, are the Happylanders considering us?

The fleet still standing by. What about our defences?

After a fortnight's delay in which the Government has again proved its utter incompetence another effort was made to evacuate Happyland by peaceful means this morning. Since it was a mere repetition of the earlier effort it was doomed to failure from the start. And fail it did.

Tom Prospect was on his way to the Mountalban building when he was stopped by the B.B.C. man. It was midday, hot, and Prospect wore his tussore suit. Flanked by Earley and Werner in linen suits, he stepped out of his custom-built Cadillac at Swan and Edgars merely from curiosity: " Always find out what's going on: that's a good motto to remember."

" Certainly is, Tom. Let's have a look-see at this set-up, eh?"

The mobile recording van had been allotted a parking space and a square-faced blond man with light tan brogue shoes trailed a microphone across the pavement in search of recordable talent. With a kind of minor desperation he lifted a finger to the engineer in the van. " Right-ho, Sid." Then to Prospect: " We're B.B.C. sir, recording impromptu opinions for our Public Opinion broadcast. Would you care to assist us?"

" Why not?" Prospect said. " I got nothing to hide."

With genial wit the blond man flicked the wisecrack into the microphone: " Here we go then, listeners. I can stooge at last. May I know your name, sir?"

Belligerently Werner said: " If you don't know that you don't deserve to be told. Why, a public personality like—"

" All right, Morrie. I aren't offended. What you want to ask me, son?"

" The matter of public interest we're dealing with to-night is the Happyland situation. What, in your view, should be the government's next step?"

With the black cigarette smoking between his fingers Prospect said in aside to Werner : "See, Morrie? You don't want to be too precipitated. If people knew who I was when I've said what I'm going to say they might think I was eating sour grapes and spittin' the pips anywhere but in my own back garden."

"You're right, Tom."

"Tom?" the blond man said. "By jove! I get it now. You're—"

With lavish humility Prospect raised his hand. "Nobody but just a member, a simple taxpaying member, of that smashing institootion the great British public. And as such it's my opinion that the sooner the government tells those brainless willies out there on Happyland that if they don't get off public property by twelve pip emma tomorrow then they can consider themselves as part of the X-bomb target, the better it'll be for everyone. Why—"

"Thank you very much indeed, sir. And now I see someone else, listeners. A lady this time. May I have your name, madam? And could you tell me briefly what you are doing in London?"

Prospect watched the woman sink into discomposure and emerge from it with desperate concern. She was a thin respectable woman in a brown dress and white cotton gloves. The gloves were her only acknowledgment of summer. After dithering and clearing her throat she said in an even respectable monotone :

"My name is Mrs. Bassett and I am in London to see a firm of people who trace people who my son Basil who is in a solicitor's office recommended me to try to see if I could trace Harold who is my other son who has disappeared it will be four months on Wednesday week."

"I see. And what are your views—"

"So when my husband said—"

" Ah, but could I butt in for a moment, Mrs. Bassett? What we really want for this broadcast is your opinion of the Happyland situation and whether you think—"

" You asked me what I was doing in London," the woman said with faded chagrin. " But if it is a matter of interfering in the lives of others I do not agree with it. I have always kept myself to myself to this day and when I saw this firm of private investigators the head of the firm suggested that my Harold might be in Happyland with his young lady even though neether Mr. Bassett or I agreed with the way Doris's father got up that petition to parliament after all she is his young lady and she might be there with him so what could we think but that these people who are pleading to have the place bombed or whatever it is are wrong. Because how could we wish that on a place where Harold might be?"

Prospect entered his car again now. " You see how selfish some people are?" he said. " Think of nobody but themselves."

" Right enough, Tom," Earley said, shifting the gear lever as the lights changed.

At the Mountalban building a small crowd was being dispersed by the police as Prospect arrived. The wooden stool on which the crowd's spokesman had stood was rolling in the gutter and every window in the now emptying street was marked by watching faces uncertain whether to register excitement, amusement or fear. High on the face of the Mountalban building a broken window hung like a black star of foreboding above the street. " Somebody feels the same way as I do, only they aren't so self-controlled." Prospect's hand gestured with secret pleasure and he ground a cigarette under his heel.

After an interval he and Earley and Werner were admitted to Mountalban's room.

"Old fashioned," Prospect said, glancing round the room. "How many times've I told you boys being old fashioned don't pay? Not even a flower in a vawse. The people expect you to have flowers—the good simple people. Why, there's the man 'imself, the very man we've come to see."

Mountalban did not rise. As if recalling something he said softly : "I too have made great capital out of a love of humanity. Sit down Mr. Prospect, Mr. Werner, Mr. Earley."

Prospect straddled the chair with his arms resting on its high back. "I see you've had visitors."

"You mean the stoning, the broken window. Yes." There was nothing at all to reveal Mountalban's feelings, not even when he said : "And did you come to gloat, gentlemen?"

"Gloat? I'm a 'umanitarian. Is that right, Walt?"

"It certainly is, Tom."

"I've done a lot for 'umanity in my time. I've given 'em jollity. That's what they want. I always said it was a crazy idea, this happiness. Leads to trouble. Bound to, when you come to think of it. Jollity's different : people can accommodate themselves to it, it's what they're used to. But anyway you've got no worry : you'll make a nice little packet out of the X-bomb. If people don't want one thing they always want another. Eh?"

"It isn't the thing I wanted to give them." Dimly Mountalban apprehended his own self-pitying sentiment. From the midst of it he plucked his original purpose and flourished it. 'Without any regard for commercial success I made a gesture to humanity.' But the inevitable success (if it didn't come from one thing it came from another; Prospect was right there) clung with fungoid tenacity to one's fingers. Automatically he looked down at his hands. "But they chose it for themselves."

161

L

Prospect grinned. " The difference between you and me is that you've got a conscience."

" I have my own spiritual standards, yes." Even as he said it he sensed the worm at the heart of things. Whatever he did he did for money. Even when, like Happyland, it was done for repentance' sake money drifted in on the tide of atonement. " But the magnitude of business is something beyond the absolute control of one individual. It's affected by—by—human nature."

" Your own first. So that what you feel now's a kind of resentment against all those good simple people who messed up your Happyland scheme with their human nature. So let 'em damn' well kid themselves, eh? Oh, I'm all for it too. I just told a B.B.C.—"

" Naturally," Mountalban said drily. " The same sort of resentment you felt against me when I opened Happyland and you thought it was in opposition to you."

Without rancour Prospect said : " I never thought a thing except about it being crazy."

" And now you know it is. Is that what you came to tell me, Mr. Prospect?"

Prospect rose. Earley and Werner rose with him. " I like people to appreciate a good bit of judgment. Morrie, give the gent a cutting."

Werner took from his briefcase a pamphlet and laid it before Mountalban.

" That's a reprint of a leader I got a friend of mine in The Street to write. Sound common sense. I 'ad a hundred thousand copies done."

When the three had gone Mountalban looked down at the pamphlet. *In the last resort even Happiness must be sacrificed to the needs of progress and security.*

He was reading the stale phrases, the pompous paraphrasing of dead platitudes when the Minister telephoned.

He didn't realise how long had elapsed since Prospect had left: his mind had been concerned with the world, humanity, himself. It got bogged down in a perplexity from which nothing at all emerged but the fact that he controlled, one way or another, an eighth of the world's commerce. It was true that the magnitude of figures had never awed him. Forgetting the telephone he said aloud: " I could escape from it today if I wished." But there was nothing to escape to. Like Satan who sorrowed on his bedside table he could achieve only hell.

" What's that?" the Minister said irritably. " I've got a bit of inside information. Everything's tied up. Gall of Harwell's ready to go ahead on the fourth. We can't resist public pressure any longer. Prospect was here an hour ago. He's as good a barometer of public opinion as any, A rough diamond—no doubt about that; but with the proverbial heart of gold. I admit he's been influencing things in the press—"

" Yes," Mountalban said, looking down at the cutting from the paper which he himself controlled and at the same time found useless, since for every editor he sacked a dozen would spring up, and denounce him if they chose or if they were paid enough.

" —but you can't still *vox populi*."

Fitch fidgeted in Mountalban's mind and he thought wearily, ' I wonder how much guilt Fitch is aware of.'

" No government can go on being flogged for ever. The people get their way in the end—er—in all the important things. After all, that's the essence of democracy. Eh? What's that?"

" I said ' what a masterpiece democracy is.' "

" Oh quite." The Minister's voice reflected his agreement. He might have invented democracy himself. " So we're sending a final ultimatum tomorrow. It's being drafted now. And if that fails our consciences will be clear. We shall have tried every way out. We shall have fought and—er—won a battle against obduracy—unjustified obduracy, I may say—the like of which has never been known. And we shall proceed accordingly. The P.M. will make a world broadcast on Wednesday at nine. That is if the Happyland people don't give in."

" And the actual bombing?" Mountalban said with cold detachment.

" On the fourth. That gives them a fortnight to change their minds even after rejecting tomorrow's ultimatum. Pretty generous, eh? And not only that : immediately prior to the bombing *another* ultimatum will be sent telling them a last-minute surrender should be signified by a Union Jack from the tower of Sumer church."

" It all sounds very reasonable," Mountalban said with the same cold detachment.

" O by George it is. And not only that, but this X-bomb affair's pretty humane, Gall tells me. No noise, no destruction—just complete silent disintegration. The opposing factor of public opinion ought to be mollified by that, don't you think?" After all, it's the—er—cruelty of weapons that makes people oppose them."

With the nearest he ever got to humour Mountalban said, " It's really quite a civilised death, eh Mr. Minister?"

After a moment's silence the Minister's voice again boomed along the wire: " By George! That's quite a thought. That's the way we'll back it, that's the line we'll take : a civilised death. That's great—great." With shadowy disappointment he added : " If we have to use it of course."

But there had never really been any doubt. *But we shall never contemplate the use of force*. It had been certain from the moment of that pronouncement. Faithlessness, iniquity, corruption, evil—they were the known qualities, their coinage was accepted everywhere, it wasn't even questioned any more. Fitch, somewhere in a dive, overhearing two men discussing a deal in rubber goods (" There'll be a market to corner, Ted; you can see the trend of things as clearly as I can. Buy now and make yourself a thousand nicker ") murmured to himself, " We live in an evil world " and longed for music. But from a loudspeaker came only a bare impersonal announcement followed by the thin spuriously weary voice of authority.

" This is London. Here is the Prime Minister, the Right Honourable—"

XII

ON the island people began to gather again, this time to listen to Loomes and de Montfort and Janet Tiptree talking to them. It was in no sense a practical gathering, since only the inmost edges of the crowd could hear what was being said, but the news would be dissembled quickly, like a flame running from mouth to mouth, and whatever was to be learnt would be learnt as quickly as when the first and subsequent ultimatums had been read.

" We have a week."

But as the warning encircled the island there was no consternation. Again without any plan being made it seemed that a course of action had been decided upon, as if what they would do was already inevitable, just as their understanding, expressed by Loomes, had been inevitable.

" You see, those left in England want to be here too; and because they cannot they feel resentment. And resentment will move people to great decisions." He looked down at the ultimatum in his hand. Vaguely in his mind stirred a reminiscence of his comprehension of the degradation to which mankind can fall without demur, can fall even with pride and justification conjured from God knows what fantastic source. But with so many years of happiness there was no real grasp. Belief in evil had faded with the years. For a moment he couldn't even believe they would bomb the island, let alone massacre the population. His eyes watched the hills and his hands touched the soil. Reality was there. Happiness was real. The threat held no terror. It was this tranquillity that he communicated to those he addressed. " For myself—" But he stopped suddenly. He had been going to say, ' I shall go on as before,' when suddenly comprehension of evil flowered out again and he knew that this time it would be impossible to go on as before. Slowly as he stood in the midst of the crowd he began to unfurl his recollection of things as they existed away from Happyland.

" You know nothing of this—this strange resentment that moves people in other lands. The memory of it has gone now. With those of you who have lived here always there is no such knowledge, forgotten or otherwise. But such evil exists. I think perhaps those of you who have been here only a little while have your knowledge of it hovering at the edge of memory, as I have. But whether we remember it or not we can no longer spurn it, we can no longer meet it with passivity, we can no longer ignore it. Because, I see now, they mean to drive us from this place by death. They believe they will not do it, that the threat is as far as they'll go, that the threat will be enough for us. They don't realise, you see, that death is no fearful thing for us. They think that till now we have been merely obstinate, that we shall hold out to the last minute and then surrender. They don't realise that vanquishment means nothing to us, that here in this happy place death is as universal as life, that it is a part, not an end, of life.

"Yes, they mean to drive us from this place by death. 'By the fear of death' they would tell you. But when they see that for us there exists no such fear, then they will extend their threat to the action itself. Resentment will become anger and anger will become fury. And fury is a strange thing—strangest in that whatever evil is its outlet there will always be a justification to turn it into good. And because of that there is always the timeless and immeasurable guilt of people consumed by what they call their fortitude, their courage, and their impeccable honesty. Because there is no shaking them in their belief in the goodness of their purpose. And in time it destroys them like a canker at the heart, even though they look on it with the eyes of a lover and call it beauty and think of it as a flower."

He stopped and looked over the vast silent crowd. Their faces, their demeanour, reflected a little anxiety now, as if he had made them concern themselves with the fate of some small creature. Harold Bassett, in the middle of the crowd, thought with sudden clarity, 'Yes: that's how people are, how we were till we came here.' With shadowy truth he saw himself and Doris as they had been. As Loomes said, a little knowledge of the other life hovered at the edge of memory. ' Why, we're not even married, yet what shame we felt we had to grope for.' Living without the grace of convention was easy because sin was unnecessary here, its attributes were invalid pelf, no-one had any use for it. He thought : ' Sin's a necessity for them over there. They must have it. They *must* live by it. Because whatever they call it—happiness, virtue, valour, it's the same hollow god stuffed with their own stupidity, their own importance, the vast immeasurable conceit that makes them believe the universe is theirs. So they're bound to worship evil and live by its rules, because that's the only way they can destroy themselves. That way the enormity of anything, *anything,* will appear justified.' Catching himself with a shadow of embarrassment in the conception of an idea he flushed.

" Guilt," Loomes was saying now. " That is the terrible thing we must bestow on them by our indifference. Guilt : that will be their heritage for countless generations. We must concern ourselves with the thought of it. Because, inevitably, even in death, we shall share it, it will be our burden too. In everything but this we can live and die without them; but, in inducing them to guilt, we too must share it. It is this that we must think of."

Doris touched her lips with an uneasy finger. It was almost the old anxiety of the life they had left. " What does he mean?"

Harold took her by the elbow. The gesture and the self-importance were familiar. " It's simple enough. He means we should consider whether or not we should sacrifice our happiness for the sake of those in England."

" You mean, go back?"

He nodded. " Everything would be the same as it was, of course."

" But this—*this*. Should we remember this?"

" I suppose so. I don't know. If we didn't—well, if we didn't it wouldn't matter. Obviously. And if we did—well, it'd be something to get nostalgic about. Like a week-end at Brighton." He was aware of the bitterness that should have been there and wasn't.

" How shall we all—" she looked with immense affection at the thousands surrounding them—" how shall we all decide?"

" The same way we decided before, I suppose. When we hoped they were just bluffing, before we faced the fact that a bluff that's called has got to be turned into a reality. Anyway, whatever decision we make it won't really be ours. Not ours as individuals. Any more than the others were. It'll be—" he gestured with his hands at the impossibility of explaining " —the island's."

The crowd again dispersed that day. The anxiety that touched them was little more than a shadow, but it was there.

Once more the ships stood by, once more the fleet of little boats surrounded the island. But the result was the same, except that this time the islanders did not even bother to unite on the shore. As the pilot of the observation plane said afterwards, " They just plain ignored us. Went on as if not a thing had happened. I went down to two hundred feet and not a one of them even bothered to look up. It was as if they just didn't know we were there; or as if, knowing, they couldn't care less."

Elaborated, that statement formed the spine of public opinion during the following week. Fitch, hopelessly listening, heard nothing but various expressions of anger. His whole world, the world of sound, seemed to be compounded of fury. In Cradle's, amid the desiccation and the humid gloom he saw a man, an elderly man, a judge of many years standing, noted for his compassion, collapse in an apoplexy of anger as he fumed at another clubman. " A week," he said with cold dispassionate bitterness, " I wouldn't give those devils out there a minute. Look at the state they've brought this country to—a maniacal . . ." but as his hands clenched and his eyes clouded he choked on the word and in a moment had collapsed.

It was the same everywhere. On the faces of people with jobs in offices and shops and neat homes with looped curtains and begonias in the garden there appeared a kind of glaze of anger. " Get on with it," they said. " Bomb the swine off."

The same festering anger flushed in headlines on every paper, and about the daily life, the commerce of England, this glow of hate hung like a furiously gathering storm.

There were still three days to go when the Minister had a solemn idea. " Even the Opposition," he thundered in the House, " are behind us—I think I dare say a hundred per cent—in our plan for dealing with the recalcitrant citizens of Happyland by reluctant force. It is, I think all hon. members of this House will agree, a plan for whose performance we can accept no responsibility, since it has been forced on us by the foolhardy populace of unhappy Happyland; it is a plan in which we have the utmost faith, believing as we do that even at the eleventh hour that pernicious populace will turn their eyes to the single gleam of sanity that remains on their horizon and capitulate to the wishes of their country by hoisting the signal of surrender in response to the final word that will be dropped from the aircraft that precedes the engine of destruction by two hours; it happily is a plan that has no ill wishes behind it, and this we have proved time and again by our efforts to evacuate the island. But it is a plan that must, gentlemen, be adhered to. I repeat—*must*. There can be no last-minute weakening of our purpose, no vacillation that would earn from the country whose interests we are solemnly pledged to regard and discharge with honour, might and glory, only the utmost contempt—a contempt that would, in my view and doubtless in the view of all hon. members, be most properly bestowed, were we unhappily to flinch at the last from our design.

" But there is, as there must always be, a small body of opinion in the country which withholds from us its approval, which prates of guilt and genocide, doubting, it would seem, the very morality of our purpose.

" Now it is not the prerogative of a democracy to judge. We can leave the judgment of thought to the totalitarian régimes whose every bitter move condemns them like stinking putrescent flesh in the nostrils of free man. Our prerogative in a democracy—and I thank God daily for it—is not to drive but to lead. And where an obviously erroneous body of thought exists we show the light, never the darkness.

" Now it has occurred to me that those who seek to accuse us of wrong-mindedness are themselves confused. They look at our plan and they see only man's purpose; and man's purpose, they argue, should be backed by God's purpose.

" It is not for me here to enter into theological argument. Heaven forbid that this House should become extended in the bounds of its accustomed controversy. But I think that those who look with dubiety on our plan for Happyland might well be won over. They might easily be won over. They might rightly be won over. The *can* be won over. They *shall* be won over."

The Minister's voice reached its histrionic peak. His hand pulled now at the cord of his monocle, then returned to his hip. On second thoughts he placed both hands on his hips. He took a small secret joy in the knowledge of his belly flattened by its new elasticated waistband. He glanced down at the smoothness of his dove-grey waistcoat. Then, seeming to bite the air a little with his malformed teeth, he went on.

" And how do I propose to win back these errant sheep who doubt our moral purpose? It is a very simple thing. And it will not only, I believe, win them back into the fold whence they have so untimely strayed but will also tend to allay any doubts that may arise in the hearts of those who with their minds proudly adhere to our rightness of thought.

"I refer, I need hardly add now, to a plan seeking the approval of the church. With such a mighty force setting its seal of approval on our plan there will, I am certain—*certain*—be ultimate unanimity.

"The church is the one great force than can convince those who doubt our moral purpose. To this end, therefore —the conviction of those who doubt our honour—I propose that a day of national prayer and dedication, with its heart in the cathedral church of Saint Paul, be held the day after tomorrow—that is, the last day before Happyland is targetised."

The Minister sat down. The murmurs of approval pleased him. His attainment of the Ministry was nothing: money and social influence had brought him the job. But applause for an idea of his own was like a consolation prize.

On the day of national prayer he attended the service of dedication in St. Paul's with the patent joy of a man who realises his own worth for the first time. The anthem and the rhetorical prayers throbbed in his head. Guilt was stilled in the lush religiosity of the church. The Minister, praying with his eyes open in order to concentrate on the spiritual richness of consecrated sanctity, noted with satisfaction the enormous peace that rested on the congregation. Faintly into the church came the echoing words of the loud-speaker system that relayed the service to the multitudes on Ludgate Hill. One was conscious of having guided people's footsteps aright. They would no longer have any doubts: it was plain in their faces, in the fervent murmurs signatory to each royally chanted prayer. 'This is my doing,' he thought with luscious pleasure.

" . . . then shall appear the wrath of God in the day of vengeance, which obstinate sinners, through the stubbornness of their heart, have heaped unto themselves; which despised the goodness, patience, and long-suffrance of God, when he calleth upon them continually to repentance . . ."

He thought vaguely of the future. There was no ambition in him : it was enough to think of himself as a humble man happy in the service of his country and appearing regularly in the photogravure supplements. Easing the creases of his trousers over his knees he watched priest and choristers and altar and the untrimmed hair of the Prime Minister in the pew in front.

" . . . If a man have a stubborn and rebellious son, which will not obey the voice of his father, or the voice of his mother, and that, when they have chastened him, will not hearken unto them : then shall his father and his mother lay hold on him, and bring him out unto the elders of his city, and unto the gate of his place; and they shall say unto the elders of his city, This our son is stubborn and rebellious, he will not obey our voice; and all the men of his city shall stone him with stones, that he die : so shalt thou put evil away from among you . . ."

How pleasing it all was, how comforting. Everyone felt the same. After the service he returned to Chelsea and waited for the mid-day papers to come in. He waited in his library, now and again taking a volume from a shelf, automatically assuming the likeness of a man of learning. With his monocle glinting he flipped the pages, murmuring to himself the proud utterances of great men, great Englishmen. His countrymen! He blew his nose in conflict with the tears of pride and straightened himself to his full stature, as though before an audience. Inadvertently he took *War and Peace* from a shelf and read aloud, carefully marking the rounded phrases, " The sum of men's

173

individual wills produced both the revolution and Napoleon; and only the sum of those wills endured them and then destroyed them." Yes. Grand stuff there too. It might almost have been written by an Englishman. It seemed to have some special relevance to the present situation too, though after the service his mind was tired and rather vague in its graspings. But it was relevant all right: his hunches were always true. He'd dig the quotation up at the apposite moment in the House.

When the papers came he himself was pictured in adequate size and in company with the P.M. The paper's leader made much of the special address. *For disloyalty to King and Country there can be only one name: treachery. And for treachery there can be only one penalty, even if the traitor is of the same blood and heritage as the betrayed.*

If thine eye offend thee . . .

So now, blessed by the grace of God, we go forward into battle, intent on no evil but only on the elimination of evil.

And across the neat towering columns the slogans bannered in still-damp and pungent ink: *No Eleventh Hour Reprieve for Happyland. Island to be targetised at noon tomorrow.*

Observers standing by.

Church asks blessing on new noiseless civilised death that is painless as a modern dental extraction.

A special contribution from the Science Editor: " Will the bomb work?"

On the children's page a painting competition was set: *Colour this drawing of the crown and arms of England— symbol of Britain's greatness—and win a post-bomb weekend for yourself and your parents in the Prospect-Before-You Camp Elysium.*

174

Idly the Minister took crayons from his desk and began to colour the drawing. It was a relief from the stress of the day, from everything. In the midst of it he called the R.A.F. station and enquired about everything. The Wing Commander was certain. " All buttoned up. The plane and the final ultimatum at H minus two."

" Talk English, please," the Minister said pontifically.

" Ten a.m. Those were my original instr—"

" Yes, yes. But a pilot . . . will there be any difficulty about a pilot?" Dimly the Minister imagined a minor mutiny throughout the air force. " Of course they'll surrender at the last minute, I'm convinced. But in case . . ."

" The pilot's detailed," the Wing Commander said with offended surprise. " Service personnel do as they're told."

" Ah, of course. Like most of us, eh?"

" In point of fact he's a newly-enlisted chappie from a civil airline. He'll remain anonymous of course. He has fuel for four hours and his instructions are to cruise over the island after he's dropped the final ultimatum—which we mustn't forget they're not expecting—until precisely eleven forty-five. Then if no flag's hoisted in surrender he's to climb to the requisite height and drop his egg. Then," the Wing Commander said with the malice of a schoolmaster repeating a statement in words of two syllables for the benefit of the class dolt—" he'll return to his base here. Minus his load."

" Yes. Yes." The Minister, the telephone abandoned, looked out on the decadent Chelsea square, heard, distantly, the clamour of a street procession moving up the King's Road. It was something the Home Secretary had sanctioned, something to do with the Martyrs of Mammon: they wanted permission to organise rescue work and carry out their missionary message, whatever it was, on targetised Happyland. No amount of explanation would convince them that if all went well there would be nothing to land on, nobody to rescue. For some heathen reason they shrank from the blessings of a civilised death weapon : they wanted blood and broken limbs and the crying of children and starvation and plague. They believed that such was man's lot, they couldn't face the fact that ideas were advancing every day. Every day.

He looked at the Tompion clock on the desk. Its glass case revealed a masterpiece of workmanship. Probably the interior of the X-bomb was like that. Precision : all in the tradition of fine British craftsmanship.

Well, by this time tomorrow it would be all over. He phoned Harwell on the secret line and spoke to Gall with a kind of juvenile excitement.

" Yes—oh, yes, everything's all right this end. The bomb itself, with a special guard, travels to the airfield tonight. There'll be a dozen of my men with it."

In sudden sweating fear the Minister said : " There's no chance . . . I mean, it isn't possible—"

" For it to go off on its journey? Oh, no. Its parts won't be fitted together until it's put on the plane; and individually they're harmless, useless. Also, it must be propelled by the velocity that only height can give. So you see you're quite safe."

" I was thinking of England," the Minister said with elaborate stoicism.

" Admirable, I'm sure."

The Minister rang off in a huff. The trouble with scientists was that they were such ill-mannered, cynical boors. But you couldn't do without them. No. They supported you all the day long of this troublous life.

The Minister went to his bedroom, removed his trousers

176

and elastic waistband and lay down to rest. On the dim edge of sleep he promised himself a holiday when all the strain was over. Perhaps a trip to New York, a visit to Avril once again. He hadn't seen her for three years. Or Hollywood. Might she be in Hollywood? Or Paris? He'd cable in the morning. 'No,' he thought, feeling the muscles of his abdomen relaxing, 'not the morning. Afternoon. Afternoon. After . . .'

When he awoke it was to find tea with lemon beside him and the Chelsea evening settling down to the smell of night-scented stock round the ragged edges of the square, the milk lorry booming down the King's Road, and the small mysterious boats moving with slow dignity between the sunlit mudbanks of the summer river. "Quite peaceful," he murmured, feeling refreshed. Then he dressed and dined at Churchill's, where the food, he thought tonight, was of surpassing excellence.

The following morning was chill in England, almost bleak. Austerely the headlines glared in the black rules. *T-day for Happyland*. The jargon and the observers' reports ran their inky way down the pages. *Fleet in the Solent. Schoolchildren to attend village services for lost loved ones.*

In the officers' mess at Haydock airfield the red-headed pilot, still twenty-two and with that agelessness of his kind, officially anonymous now and segregated from his brother pilots by something that none of them could have defined, scanned the pages of successive newspapers with his amazed and childlike eyes. On the woman's page of the *Express* he discovered a recipe and recited the ingredients and method with a kind of hopeless relief. "I wonder they don't call it Crucifixion Cake." But the bitterness wasn't real: it was calculated, dispassionate. Nonetheless the mess emptied and the red-headed boy was left alone.

177

M

His briefing was incised in his mind. He had no need to dwell on it. He spent no thought on it at all. He remembered how as a child he'd filled the day of his visit to the dentist with the thought of a cup final, so that right up to the moment of the finger on the dentist's bell there had miraculously been nothing at all to fear. He was capable of immense and effortless concentration and he concentrated now : on the echo of a conversation with Tom Prospect. ' Then we set out to smash the real thing up because we're afraid of it.' With the same contrived bitterness he said it again and again, believing in it to hide the horror of what was beyond belief.

Once in the air he twisted the horror away from him by the same dispassionate concentration. There were the two release buttons beneath his finger, and the synchronised clock, and the fuel indicator with four hours' fuel. And of course the whole trip would be unnecessary. The last-minute surrender would come, he knew the tower of Sumer Church so well, he knew precisely where to hover . . . " Para," he read from the black button, and imagined the yellow silk swooning gently to earth; and " Load "—but he made imagination boggle at that.

It was not until he was over the island and shouting aloud in the small imperilled space of the cockpit that he began to realise a horror even greater than the action for which he had been sent.

" Jubilate !" he shouted, conjuring the word from God knew where. " Good old jubiloobilate ! Happylanders here I come !" His voice was enormous in this own ears. Bitterly he cried aloud to the dials and rushing air, " Oh, you silly bloody fools." The useless dead phrases of schoolroom and pub came spinning back : " I have no pain now mother dear, but Oh, I am so thirsty. Dear mother I am on the road to ruin, please meet me half-way."

But it lasted only a moment. "Over target," he said coldly into the microphone. "H minus two hours five minutes. Cloud high, sun bright, conditions okay."

Poised over the island with huge and death-like precision he began thinking, 'They'll see me as a vulture, waiting to plunge.' With the telescopic sight he observed people in the fields. Going down, sundering the air with the noise of his descent, he glimpsed (or thought he glimpsed : it was the same thing) a child in a red dress—running, screaming. Or was it something inside himself he heard? He flattened the plane at a thousand feet and rose again, banking westward, with the button pressed and the sweat streaking his newly-lined and awful aged flesh in runnels.

"Parachute away," he whispered into the microphone, tasting the salt on his rigid lips.

The yellow silk flowered beneath him and as he banked and climbed he thought of the horror they would feel, seeing it fall, believing it death, 'But of course they wouldn't feel that—not in a happy place.' He tried to recall happiness from his own experience there, but it was beyond recall. What he felt—and now in sweating agony he at last acknowledged it—was not the horror of the death it was in his power to inflict, but of the dreadful exaltation.

"Happylanders here I come!" The words tore away as he dived again. It was joy. The island spun to meet him and he thought with icy calculation within the exaltation, 'After . . . I'll wreck the kite' and he thought of the enveloping tower of cool green water "The things I've done for England."

He climbed again now, noting automatically that the parachute had landed . . . somewhere . . . in the midst of fields. "Where my parachute has rested," he chanted. "Somewhere among the happiness"—thinking with sudden rapture of a butterfly making its bright blue way across the tumultuous Swale as he watched from Richmond Hill with a brunette schoolgirl whose name he'd forgotten and of whom the only thing he remembered was that she said, " If only I had Coral Bowen's latin grammar : she's got all the answers in there. All of them. Every one."

He invoked memories in terror, invoking them as a balm, feeling them cool him. But they lasted such a little time and somehow his store of them was beyond real touch : only scraps flicked at him.

He circled the island, flying low. The clock marked off two minutes and he thought, ' Two hours. Then I shall be free. Then I can drop it.' It was a kind of awful radiant joy, the bitter lust of unbounded power; and he knew suddenly that he didn't want them to surrender, that this, this dreadful evil joy, was what he had been horrified at. But now, in the admission, horror passed and itself became joy. He was suddenly cool again and quite intent. " No signal."

" No signal." His words came back to him. Somewhere at the airfield a message was going out : " H minus one hour forty-eight minutes and no response to final ultimatum." He heard it clicking across the countless miles, the secret lines masking the news that, like the score in some game of great moment, would be made public immediately.

" No signal."

He cruised now, letting the joy flood through him. There wasn't any point in kidding yourself it was horror when really it was exaltation. ' This is what the torturers feel,' he thought—' the Belsen mob, the yobs who burn animals alive, those who rape and those who lynch and those who observe with glee when there is someone to crucify; and maybe because they feel it and because everyone else is halfway to feeling it all the time—maybe that's why the world—'

Banking, he turned and crossed the island from east to west. He was at nine hundred feet and he went down to five hundred, thinking of the noise as it would be heard on the island.

He picked out the church easily and as he circled he glimpsed people running. 'Don't let them surrender,' he prayed, and began to climb again, thinking of his briefing, reading off the tablets in his mind 'Like Moses and the jolly old commandments.' *You will climb to three thousand feet and from there you will ensure that the camera maga-zine is charged and the motor turning. With the central landmark at zero in your sights and with the proper allow-ances made for the speed and wind and altitude you will release your load at noon precisely. It is expected that the complete disintegration of the target will be accomplished in something under three minutes. During the period you will remain in flight over the island with your camera in action and at the end of it you will return to base.*

'Three minutes,' he thought. 'All that land and all those people—*non est* in three minutes. Like Jules Verne.'

In the morning papers, probably, some enterprising journalist would write ponderingly of the thought of the pilot who released the X-bomb. *His anonymity is preserved, but we can imagine him as a family man with two or three children and a rose garden. He probably smokes a pipe and makes a jaunt to the local for a pint and a game of darts every night. And his thoughts at that solemn moment of pressing the release button? Who can tell? It can only be said that they dwelt, as an Englishman's should, on service to his country.*

He laughed, quite softly, thinking of the people down below. 'Swine. Not even needing to pray. Maybe even

181

welcoming a happy death. Why the hell should *they* have it? Why? Ah.' he thought cunningly, ' it ought to be a bomb that hurts. They'd pray then.'

He flew westwards ten miles and turned and flew in again over the island, screaming against the wind. It was the simple bullying malice of a schoolboy that moved him then. The hour to go (it had dwindled, even time had dwindled) till noon would be like a history of increasing malice. ' Noise. Scream over the top of them now, low. Give 'em a foretaste. Make 'em wonder.'

Once again he circled the island, banked and rose.

" No signal."

But he hadn't looked. He feared to look now.

" H minus forty-seven minutes."

" How simple they make it,' he thought. ' Only living and dying are difficult. Death they make so simple.'

But now, climbing once again, colder, cold as death beneath the sweat that had soaked the lambswool collar of his jacket and was still falling drop by drop from his eyebrows in quiet incessant motion onto his cheeks, he wondered thoughtfully, ' Can I do it?' Because he didn't trust his brain much longer. ' In forty minutes,' he thought dispassionately, ' I think I may be mad. Quite cracked. Dotty.'

When he took off his glove (' I shall need the glove off to press the button ') and slid his hand across his face it was like drawing it through a film of grease. And in his hands and head a column of vivid blood seemed to be pounding. He wondered without surprise if it were blood that bathed his face, but when he looked at his hand it was quite unmarked save by the channels of dirt and the map of his character, his life, his human majesty. ' Thirty-nine minutes. No: I can't wait that long.'

Climbing this time he watched the altimeter. He was thinking of the green column of water, the endlessness of it, the enveloping power and peace. The horror returned again and with it a moment's clarity.

" Happylanders here it comes. Early. Aren't you jubilant? Joobiloobiloobilant? Getting death before dishonour, death before noon, forty minutes and two-fifth seconds before you're supposed to have it? Just because. A whim. A little pilot's whim. Little Ginger's whim.'

He was all right now. All right. " Happylanders here I come:" it fitted the *California* tune a treat. Dead right. Dead. Dead in the sight. Landmark dead in the sights. Three thousand. There it was on the meter. Flicker, flicker. Dead on. Bank. Turn. Landmark . . .

The island tilted beneath him, its shape and verdure clear. For a moment he thought of cutting the engines, feeling the silence, the space. But silence would have been unbearable. Like guilt in the night. So no silence.

The engines shattering the world with their sound. ' And me in the midst.'

He climbed for a run in and watched the altimeter, then watched the island tilt away again in the telescopic sights.

" Here we go," he said gently as with his free hand he felt for the button, the red one, his flesh identifying the engraved word " load," as he dropped, wondering with awful fear is he would be able to summon, from the depths of his body, the strength to give it pressure; and wondering too if—

But he would never recall now what he wondered in that moment. Because from the squat tower of Sumer church, the chosen landmark, the sign of vanquishment was flying; and all the dreadful exaltation was suddenly dead in his heart.

Then he turned and flew eastward, home.

XIII

ALL along the south coast the people from Happyland were being landed. With a proper and serious-minded regard for preparation against any eventuality all the necessary arrangements had been made beforehand, and the coastal towns were taking a civic pride in their ability to cope.

At Portsmouth a sloop tied up at the hards on the last day of the landings and the hundred or so Happyland evacuees who were that ship's burden came ashore about noon. They came slowly up from the hards, following the arrows to the medical huts—men to the left, women to the right, they couldn't go wrong.

The doctors sat on wooden forms, their stethoscopes swinging from their necks, their bored warm hands touching each man's genitals as they listened without interest to the accompanying coughs, shining their torches into the recesses of armpit and groin as they instructed their orderlies to spray the D.D.T. But there was no disease: no rabies or pox or *noli-me-tangere* marred the population of Happyland; no common colds stuffed their noses, no rheumatism cramped their limbs; only as occasional pregnancy demanded notation on S.O. Form H. Evac/Ldg 49P (8).

The doctor at Table 39 in the women's hut took the identity card of her last examinee. " Doris Cheesman," she quoted at her orderly. " Got it?"

" Yes, Doctor," the orderly said, writing it on the form clipped to her desk.

" Relax," the doctor said. Doris lay on the couch, feeling the stethoscope's finger probing across her chest. She

184

hoped the doctor wouldn't notice the way she'd flushed up : it was a kind of arch shame at what she believed the doctor might notice.

The doctor did of course. " Last period?"

" I—er—I don't actually know . . . Time . . . we lost count of it—"

" Near enough?" the doctor pressed impatiently.

" I reckoned up about nine weeks."

" Feeling all right? Sickness? Tenderness round the nipples?"

" A bit. I don't know . . . I think—"

" Nothing to think at all. Quite in order. I'll give you authority for milk, orange juice, halibut liver oil. Keep the bowel free. Liquid paraffin." Signing the form she turned to the orderly. " That really is the last then. Glory be to God. Now perhaps I shall be able to give some attention to people who need it. England's complete population is now in circulation again." She looked up at Doris who had dressed and was standing before the table. " Yes?"

" I don't know . . . my name on the identity card . . . it's different now—I'm Doris Bassett; at least—well, I'm not really, perhaps; but I sort of got married on Hap—"

The doctor turned from the portable basin where she was washing her hands. " Your name's not really any concern of mine : only your health. Try the registration hut. They'll do whatever's necessary."

She watched Doris go out. " Thinks I worry about how where and why she conceived." Wearily she took off her white coat and stood revealed in neat blue serge and beige shirt. " What on earth *is* happening to all these people?"

But the question was rhetorical. Now that the last had passed before her she felt free from concern. In any case the answer was plain if you glanced at any newspaper, listened to any radio bulletin. There were rehabilitation centres all over the south for those who had nowhere to go. The Minister had summed the matter up as he considered admirably in a speech to the House the day following the surrender of Happyland.

". . . they have surrendered. Our cause is won. Right has triumphed as right must always triumph. Our navy is now bringing our errant citizens back to this land, and is bringing too the entire original population of Happyland—some hundred thousand souls.

" My hon. friend opposite asks me what is going to happen to all these people. I reply, in the knowledge that I have full justification for saying so, that I neither know nor care—at least in my official capacity. Part of my task is done : I have secured the surrender of Happyland. It is for my colleague in the Home Office to answer the hon. member's question. He, no doubt, in the fullness of his efficiency, has all his plans laid. For myself, I must now re-dedicate such poor talents as I possess to the remainder of my task that still lies ahead.

" For I must remind the House that it is the testing of the X-bomb that is my main responsibility. I have thrust aside the barrier that the Happyland crisis put in the way of this great experiment, but the bomb is still untested.

" As the House knows, the last-minute surrender caused the targetisation of Happyland to be postponed, since however bitter we may have felt in mind we could not in the mercy of our spirit do ought but stay our hand at the plea for mercy of the islanders.

" The subsequent evacuation, organised to combat muddle and disease, has taken three days. And the world, unconcerned in our domestic affair of recalcitrant citizens, waits impatiently the news of our success with an experiment that affects, I dare swear, every man, woman and child who breathes today, plus tomorrow's untold generations.

"I must, then, as the House is fully aware, forge ahead with my task. Further postponement of the targetisation of Happyland can no longer justifiably be supported. I therefore leave the question of the hon. member opposite unanswered, for the simple reason that the answer is not for me to give, and refer him to my colleague in the Home Office."

The Home Secretary's reply, his analysis of the needs of the evacuated population of Happyland, was published two days after Harold Bassett and his Doris arrived at Portsmouth. They read it in the communal dining-room that had once been a Methodist chapel and which bore still the remnants of an atmosphere of Edwardian Sundays and fiery sermons that harboured strangely the bewilderment of a defeated people.

"Happyland," Harold Bassett said; and there again on the crumpled sheets the word appeared; and heading the gossip columnist's diary was the likeness of Mr. Mountalban—the same file photograph showing the sparse hair and clerkly spectacles, the same contrived mystery spread down the column : *" I have no statement to make " was all that could be elicited even by this column's most seductive methods.*

"Happyland," Doris repeated after him. " What will they do with us now?"

" Do with us?' His inflexion was of dignity maintained. It was a dignity strangely culled from a tradition he had derided so often, laughing with controlled humour at stiff upper lips. "Nothing, naturally. We're not theirs to command. They can only provide for material needs, food and lodging and the like." The pipe carefully pointed the words. " After all, they're morally bound to do that. But we're as free in spirit as ever we were. We're not refugees, you know."

But of course they were. Justice, mercy and affection were produced like endless ribbons from the hat momentarily doffed by public opinion. *The British quality of mercy is not strained* was the Home Secretary's text. *Our task is enormous but it is not impossible. I summon British humour and British phlegm and British vigour as the vanguard. With these three mighty warriors at our head let us go forward together.*

Now as to practical details the published statement continued. *On statistical analysis we find that the actual number of persons evacuated from Happyland was* 525,723. *Of these* 113,611 *have returned to the homes from which they departed and propound no further problem. Of the remaining* 412,112, 100,107 *are the original population of Happyland, and for these, naturally, no homes exist in this country. For them His Majesty's Government accept full responsibility; for them full arrangements were already made in the original evacuation plans. But for the remainder, some* 312,000 *souls, it was considered neither necessary nor desirable to make plans. These people drew out their savings, sold up their houses—even, in many cases, breaking up their families—and left this country in the foolhardy pursuit of a happiness to which they had no right. It ill becomes them to fall now upon the charity of their countrymen whom, without a shred of consideration they left ' in the lurch.'*

Nonetheless the British quality of mercy will not let them suffer unduly, and, under a pressure of public opinion with which I began by being in indignant disagreement and have now, perhaps by virtue of my own inherent quality of

*mercy, come to see in a juster light, I have made the
necessary arrangements for the re-establishment of some
of the old army camps as rehabilitation quarters.*

*This, as must be clear, is, and can be, only a temporary
measure. The vast majority of these people are not only
homeless but penniless too, and many of them may have
great difficulty in getting new employment, since their em-
ployers—not unreasonably—filled the vacancies caused by
their absence. But it is, and I state it with the greatest possible vigour, entirely up to them to remould their lives from
now on. We can aid individual cases only on their merits:
the majority must be done by as the exigencies of adminis-
tration permit; and to this end I have empowered local
boroughs and urban districts to accommodate, sustain and
nourish those of the ex-Happyland population who are
thrust upon them, in a manner similar to that tended to the
blamelessly destitute and the vagrants of the realm.*

" Vagrants," Doris said. " Is that what we are now?
Tramps?"

They were in the queue that led to the Registration
Officer's table. " Don't talk ridiculous." Harold put down
the bright tan suitcase and flung his trench coat across his
shoulder; then he took his wallet from his breast pocket.
The little doll was still in his lapel and the rubber bulb
hung down with a kind of obscene suggestion. " We've still
got a bit of money." He tapped the wallet and replaced it
and the rubber bulb in his pocket. " We're leaving here
now."

" But what—"

" We've got initiative, haven't we? Brains?"

" I suppose so." Almost happily she abandoned herself
to masculine domination. Of course Hal would look after
her. Weren't they man and wife?—in the sight of God,
anyway.

They came to the table. The man who sat there had a ginger moustache. " Name?"

" Harold Bassett and Doris Cheesman."

" Are you married or sister and brother or what?"

" Friends—just friends." He wanted to imply all that the word would mean to a man of the world, but the man didn't seem to catch on.

" Want accommodation? Sustenance?"

" No. Charity's something we don't accept." He tried to make the words biting, but they were only tentatively humiliated.

" All right then. No need to keep you. Next."

Behind them in the queue was Brutus Robinson; and behind him Loomes. Harold Bassett took *Transcendental* from his pocket and tore a leaf from it and wrote in the margin *Mount Royal, Marble Arch.* With a condescension in which he seemed to take a great pride he said : " We'll be at this address—for a night or two, anyway. Come and see us if you're in difficulties." Then he picked up the suitcase and walked quickly to the door. Doris beside him, her hand apologetically linked in his crooked elbow.

" Whatever did you say that for? We shan't be there, shall we?"

" Why not? We've got to be somewhere."

" But Mount Royal! It's so—so—" but no suitable word would come and she had to choose one she knew he'd detest : " Posh."

He didn't answer. As if to punish her he didn't speak till they reached Winchester. With a kind of induced desperation he tried in silence to recapture happiness, but nothing remained. It was like trying to force a dream to the surface. And when he looked sideways at Doris, at the unreal ivory profile and the stamped gold medallions of her hair he saw that for her too there was only bewilderment. But at least she'd have the child. For himself, he felt beneath the puzzlement and the elaborate self-consciousness only a deep sense of hurt, almost of sorrow—the nostalgia of a child fugitive from home in a dark wood, his courage gone. Dimly he apprehended that the elaborate learning laid bare only the tiny platitude; it was like seeking the answer to two and two in the Theory of Relativity.

But the moment of timely humility quickly passed: it was a quality against which his spirit eternally fought. The taste acquired from other people, the opinions quoted as his own, the false face of knowledge—they crowded everything else out, made the battle uneven. It was too late now, one's character was formed, one accepted the finished production with a sneer and derided it in others. There was comfort in the assurance that if you could laugh at yourself you were all right.

" Back to this," he said, peering from the window. Outside a country station a poster peeled. *Happyland*—the word in its once-luminous print faded to the colour of mud, and at Waterloo the electric newspaper unwound its ribbon of dotted words : NAVAL DESERTER TO HAPPYLAND TO BE COURT-MARTIALLED. Yes, they were back again. Desperately he squeezed the doll's rubber bulb and a tiny stream of brackish water (how long since he'd filled it?) squirted out. " Dreadful thing. Can't think why I ever bought it. I suppose one must put on a paper hat and sing foolish songs occasionally." He ripped the doll from his lapel and flung it into a litter basket as they left the station.

" Harringay," Doris read from a poster. " Look— Eileen Joyce is still playing. Four concertos in one evening. You wouldn't think she could do it, would you? She's so delicate-looking."

He could see she felt secure and comforted. The buses to Tooting Bec ran at ten-minute intervals and he sensed her longing to board one. (But of course she was his now : she wouldn't dream of suggesting it.) They'd been happy once : the proof of their happiness had made a national crisis. " Well, now we're just ordinary people."

" I wonder if they all feel the same?"

He recollected the actual happenings on Happyland so clearly. Only the spell, the enchantment, was broken. The dream would not break the surface. Right up to the moment of their departure everything was clear. Even the decision to surrender, Loomes saying quietly over and over again, " We must spare them their guilt in order to avoid our own;" and de Montfort's bewilderment over the matter of the flag : " Flag? We have no flag. What is the purpose of such a thing?" Robinson had said, " Naturally they think we possess a union flag. They need its symbolism to hold them together. But they will understand equally a bit of white cloth. That also is symbolic." It was Loomes who had fixed it to the tower, who had by his action absolved them from guilt, stolen from them possibility of death in the midst of Happiness. But, like enchantment, resentment too was dead.

They stayed three days at Mount Royal, enjoying the privileged luxury, ordering tea and sweet cakes by telephone to room service, believing they avoided the mannerisms of suburban newlyweds.

Happiness was lost, but they had a compensatory pleasure : " Well, we've dared and done." They sat in the park and Harold summoned every contempt as he watched the familiar spectacle of dreary family life—the harassed mothers, the nagged fathers, the sticky unwanted children. " We've avoided *that*."

Shame loomed in Doris' mind but she ignored it for his

sake, for her own. "You mean we could leave each other if we wanted?"

"Well, we're not married, are we?"

"But we almost were."

"That isn't the point."

The pipe came out and he filled it with slow deliberation. "We agreed to be, and we swore we'd never let it collar us like that, like that family there trying to find a bit of relaxation in a world of monotony. But it might have been too strong for us—the coils of convention spring tight once you're inside them." He sat back with the air of a wit who has achieved an epigram. "We'd probably have let ourselves be conquered. Whereas now—" He looked at her somewhat devilishly. "It's like a Noël Coward situation— Design for Living. I'd love to see the old parents' faces— and Basil's and Arthur's. Imagine their horror! 'Living in sin! And her, the brazen hussy—going to have a baby.' Jezebel, my dear. You'd be Tooting Bec's Jezebel."

"I suppose we'll never go back there?"

He missed the note of tentative hope in her voice. "Not bloody likely. Well—maybe for an hour or so one Sunday afternoon, just to shake 'em up a bit. Can't you imagine their faces, the aspidistras with the eyes watching from behind, the curtains twitching? God! what an adventure."

Yes, at least they'd dared and done. His pride and pleasure were enormous. He credited himself with the avoidance of the dreadful burden of conventionality, and with raising Doris from the morass of sentimentality in which she'd been floundering cheerfully.

"We'll enjoy ourselves a bit," he said, poking at his wallet. "Still a few quid left." There was a distinct triumph in this new enjoyment, this surreptitious daring. ("I bet even the reception clerk doesn't twig we're not married.")

On the second day Loomes and Robinson came to see

N

them. " Come up to our suite," Harold Bassett said. " We can talk in privacy there."

The small room had only two chairs but Harold and Doris sat on the beds. " Come to compare experiences?"

" Not quite that, I think," Loomes said. " We too lost our happiness. We too are ordinary people now." He was thinking of the original people of the island, those who had never known anything but happiness, and how they had been swept up in the tide of surrender. " For Brutus Robinson and me it's just a return to something we have known before—even if we had all but forgotten it; but for those others . . . they must be finding it very strange."

" O, they're all right," Harold Bassett said. " No worse off than us. I read in the paper only yesterday that the government's starting up training centres for them everywhere, hope to make useful citizens of 'em yet. It's the others, the ones who gave up their homes, that I feel concerned about." His concern evaporated in thin blue pipe smoke above their heads. " Of course you wouldn't know, but there was a housing shortage before this Happyland business. Then, with so many going over there, selling up, it eased the shortage. Now people have come back the shortage is on again."

Brutus Robinson took a paper from his pocket. " A week ago we were treated as bitter enemies. Now, it seems something must be done." The banner headline flared across the columns : *Something Must Be Done*. The dimly noble phrases of the journalists limped down the columns : *They were our enemies . . . now vanquished . . . temper justice with mercy . . . finest attribute of the British character . . . pending the inauguration of bigger schemes by the Government this newspaper fearlessly pleads for help from its readers . . . gifts of clothes, food and money . . . expected that Mr. Eric Mountalban may launch a fund . .*

194

"Yes, we're like that—dotty but nice" Again pride and pleasure stirred in Harold Bassett; and again mockery came up in combat: "If only we could see how ridiculous we looked to others." With sudden concern he said: "What are *you* going to do?"

"Money," Loomes said. "We shall need that, it seems. Before anything. There must be a living somewhere—a large vicarage, a small stipend."

"A little publicity," Harold Bassett said with deliberation. "That's what you need. Why, the notoriety alone . . . You want to go and see one of those newspapers, write for them—'Why I surrendered' by the Parson of Happyland."

"They got in touch with me. I promised I'd let them know."

"You might as well have said yes in the first place. It's the only way you'll make any money. Large rectories and small stipends are no longer—er—economic possibilities. The cost of living's gone up a bit since you left England. You'll have to get into line."

"Yes: into line. Perhaps Mr. Mountalban—"

"Or Lord Prospect," Robinson said. "After all, they both owe us . . . well, sustenance."

"You could sing." The light brown eyes achieved a patent humour. "They're bound to need singers at Elysium. Or entertainers—story-tellers. You ought to get a job doing that. You old devil." The pipe came out and poked Robinson in the chest. "Kidding us . . ." Harold Bassett looked round with surreptitious pleasure at the hotel room, thinking of their names in the register and of the way they'd cocked a snook at that symbol of respectability. "However, we aren't altogether worried—as you see." The eye winked, the pipe withdrew.

"O, that." Robinson turned to Loomes. "You might

195

almost think they took a pride in sinfulness." He began to sing softly a phrase of *Wachet auf, ruft uns die Stimme*, probing for the words that, like happiness, had got lost in memory. His eyes glinted with amusement, but it was amusement of a thin and spurious kind, like an echo. " I think you may be—" but he paused, as if it wasn't yet the right time to say what he'd intended to say.

" We've even started a family," Harold Bassett said now with the furtive boldness of a commercial traveller beginning a smutty story in the hearing of a woman he's not quite sure of.

Searching back in memory Loomes found the appropriate conventionality. " Congratulations."

" Thanks." He felt really devilish, bohemian. He walked in imagination down a vista of admiration : ' Nothing staid about old Harold Bassett . . . don't blame him . . . you've got to hand it to his type—they do what they want . . . not like a lot of sheep . . . living, living—he's made an art of living . . . doesn't care a damn for anyone.' "

" Well," Loomes said. " We must be on our way."

Harold stood up. He was suddenly the good fella, a one for a good turn. He took a note from his wallet. "Here."

On Loomes' face there was a smile. " Thank you—no. It wasn't necessary. We shall manage. We came thinking *you* might need help. Not money of course . . . but a word, perhaps a gesture. We were very good friends . . . over there"

Harold Bassett felt himself flushing and bit angrily on his pipestem. " No, thanks. I've got a job I can go back to—if I want. But I'm on my own from now on. I've got a brain, initiative."

" And an immortal soul, too. We'll meet again. I feel

we're bound to." Loomes looked across London from the window, his eyes embracing the world. " We're in the same net—"

" —and it's a small world." Harold Bassett didn't bother to repress the sneer.

In the doorway Brutus Robinson said : " I had a sister. She married into royalty—one of the Balkan kings. I must look her up. She's probably still at Claridge's."

" You're as likely to find her there as anywhere else, no doubt." Harold Bassett skipped neatly from the pit of humiliation. " Or maybe you could go back to your job in the time-making factory—you old kidder!"

From the pocket of his soiled shirt Robinson took a slip of paper. " Something I found when I was going through my belongings before I left the island. All useless things. I abandoned them all. But this I thought might be of interest to you."

He and Loomes went out. They could be heard descending the stairs, having ignored the lift as unnecessary to men who had legs and plenty of time.

" Old devils—both of 'em." Humility had given way to bonhomie now. Well, perhaps it had been a shade off taste, offering them a pound like that. He wasn't going to harbour any resentment anyway.

" What does it say?" Doris moved over to him.

" This?" He lit his pipe deliberately, holding the cutting against the heel of the hand that grasped the pipe. " We'll see, shall we? Probably the original of his tale about the tadpole."

But it wasn't. It was a cutting from *The Times,* faded thin at the fold, giving a list of new ordinations *Announced from Lambeth Palace last night.* At the head of the list was the name Brutus Robinson, M.A.

" But what's it mean?"

197

After a moment he said : " Mean? It means we're tied up—spliced. Properly. It means he's a real parson. That's what it means. That's all."

As he watched her relief he managed to summon a feeling of distaste that satisfied the dead derring-do. But it was relief that he too felt. Secretly he reached for the surreptitious false joy of the illicit hotel bedroom; but it had faded, gone. The backyard fences were closing in, the daily job loomed big, there was no longer any need to ask at the bookstalls for *Transcendental* or at the libraries for Kant. Even the Buffaloes were not impossible now. Arthur and Basil would have the last laugh. " Love in a furnished room," he said with the last remnants of distaste.

" But Hal—Hal, it doesn't matter !" Her eyes were quite full of joy as she flicked the final platitude at him. " We love each other."

Slowly he rolled the cutting into a spill, lit it and held it to his pipe, imagining for a moment that its revelation wasn't theirs, that they would lie happily ever after on a bed of sin. ' If only we hadn't known. We could have gone on always, believing . . .' But knowledge had dragged them by the hair back to the life they belonged to. There was no escaping it.

XIV

FITCH went up the stairs slowly, settling his stomach, acknowledging the nods of the desk-and-telephone men, amused at their petty aloofness. " I am on my way to Mr. Mountalban "—and he imagined their reaction, ' What news does the old buzzard bring this time?' Yes, undoubtedly they thought of him as a spectre, a picker of flesh at life's feast.

" I seek sanctuary—sanctuary." And there it was: the quiet, beautiful room with his master behind the walnut desk, the tape machine issuing its news with minute tickings.

" Sanctuary, Mr. Fitch? From what?"

Carefully he turned the desk-light away from his eyes. " One is always seeking sanctuary from the consequences of one's actions." His literary phrases were good today. " The bomb. Of course the bomb."

Mountalban crossed his ankles, eased his neat striped trousers above the grey spats. " Everywhere I go people look intense, fearful. I don't know why. My newspapers constantly assure them of the facts. The bomb is harmless outside the prescribed area of its target. It's a good thing I'm not a man easily angered, Mr. Fitch. People insult me by implication—they seem to doubt that the industries I control, the scientists whose salaries I pay, the physicists whose laboratories I equip, are capable of making the bomb they've promised. Gall has assured me, categorically, that there will not even be a sound. Nobody will hear anything."

" Perhaps, conceivably, an echo." Fitch took from his pocket an antique watch and stood it against the base of the lamp. " Twenty minutes to twelve. The destruction of Happyland, the newspapers say, will take place at noon." He leaned back and folded his hands. " A quiet death, a civilised death. The columnists in the papers are beginning to call it 'the well-mannered bomb.' Death is at last a civilised thing, they tell us."

Mountalban wrote a neat sum in figures on the corner of his memo pad, then laid the threepenny pen in the jade pen tray. " But nobody is dying, Mr. Fitch. The place is

199

empty. Nobody at all is dying." He spoke gently, tonelessly. "You're a little . . . overwrought" He moved over to the ticker. British Atomic Piles. Corrugated Steel Corporation. A few more figures on the pad. "What news have you for me, Mr. Fitch?"

But for a moment Fitch could not speak. He had walked from Bloomsbury and had been aware of moving in the very heart of a waiting world. Despair riddled the dead heart like maggots, but it was plastered over with the journalists' wishful observation, the statesman's weary hope. In a store people huddled round a television screen like animals seeking warmth, and The Brigade mounted guard in the Palace quadrangle as the traffic rolled by and sightseers gaped at the window where the king appeared fleetingly with his hands behind him.

In a milk bar in Haymarket Fitch asked for a glass of hot water and heard a girl whisper to her companion : "It's awful, but ever so exciting. Messenger's given me an extra half-hour to hear the radio commentary. You can't believe that island'll just vanish, can you?"

"It's wonderful what they do nowadays," the other girl said.

Fitch moved on. He couldn't get out of his mind that it was the end of the world. But in Fortnum's a girl in a pale blue overall was stacking china pots of caviare and an American snapped Eros with a Leica as the Guinness clock marked off the minutes. *After the X-bomb— what?* a placard read and Fitch asked the question aloud. *The world waits for noon.* Dramatized, the event smeared the world's rotting heart with excitement. People moved on, enjoying it, each aware of his own despair and feeling it unique. But not Fitch. Invective failed him and compassion was something he had never known. There was only fear.

He moved up Shaftesbury Avenue on the shady side,

seeking the Choral Symphony—it was supposed to have a message of hope, but he thought of Beetoven's bitter irony and the spirituality with which he had burdened a world unprepared.

In the gramophone shop the proprietor came forward immediately. " Mr. Fitch, what a pleasure to see you. Such a long time . . ."

Over in the tiny audition room the enormous crescendos of the Ninth battled with his horror but he couldn't concentrate and he emerged after ten minutes with the discs in his hand. " I'm afraid . . . I can do the music no justice."

" Disturbing times," the proprietor said. " Perhaps another time. I have a unique Battistini; I'm keeping it for you. I'll tell Mr. Bassett to take special care—"

" That young man? He's back then?"

" Not yet. But he's been to see me. Been out on that island of course. People like you and me, Mr. Fitch, those who held the fort . . . But one mustn't be hard. As the paper says, the British quality of mercy . . . So I gave him his job back He needs it. He's a family man now, it seems —or will be in a few months. ' Foolish,' I told him, ' in such disturbing times.' But you can't convince the young. So I gave him his job back—on the understanding that his first week's wages goes to the fund."

" Fund?" Fitch said.

" The ' Save the Happylanders ' affair. You know the Lord Mayor—"

" Of course. Yes, the Happylanders. I'd forgotten—"

Waggishly the proprietor shook a finger. " But one shouldn't forget, Mr. Fitch. After all, in the sight of God they are our brothers."

" Yes. They are our brothers. No: I shan't forget Happyland. If only—"

" But the Government had to do *some*thing, Mr. Fitch. It wouldn't have been possible to keep adding to that vast number of people without introducing starvation, disease. If you ask me, they nipped it in the bud just in time. Goodness only knows what it would have come to in a while ... completely out of hand. Why, I'm not a covetous man, but I was beginning to be inflamed by the desire to go there myself. It's a strange feeling—this longing for happiness."

With his ears pricked against the wind of rumour he walked westward once more. But this morning there was no rumour to be heard in the open streets (it was all fact there : " Well, the balloon goes up at twelve ") and he hadn't the courage to seek the places where it might be found. In his jester's loneliness he wanted to be with his king, he felt that to be alone would be more than he could bear; and guilt as well as fear could be shared.

But Mountalban said only, " What news have you for me, Mr. Fitch?"

Maliciously he said : " Your name doesn't head the list of contributions to the fund."

" That is the king's privilege, Mr. Fitch." Still his voice was toneless, quite cold. " Besides, there is a dignity about it being at the foot of a subscription list : it gives the effect of a cornerstone."

Fitch took up his watch and held it close to his face. " Ten minutes."

" I am giving twenty-five thousand pounds to the ' Save the Happylanders,' Mr. Fitch. Does that restore my prestige in your eyes? All the time, you see, one is throwing good money after bad. One cannot deal with humanity at all. They have no respect, no pity."

" Ah, you want to be pitied because you—"

" Not a bit, Mr. Fitch, not I. Pity is a loathsome thing. But they are worthy of it and I give it to them—twenty-five thousand pounds' worth. Because I—I hate them; and there is nothing quite so degrading, so humiliating, as living on the charity of your late enemies. Our human brothers. Given the world, they fight and excrete in it like animals. Given happiness, the one priceless thing, they—" He stopped and made another note on his pad. " The Fund will be a great success. Everybody likes giving to the dog they've kicked to death. I too. I find an immense satisfaction in it, Mr. Fitch." He looked carefully at the clock. " And at noon I shall kick them all to death again."

Fitch started. His eyes blurred with tears and he could think of nothing but the cheering words of the Wayside Pulpit : *Misfortune knocks at the door to see what you are made of.* " I knew," he murmured. The bladder was pricked, the jests had been squeezed from the jester now. " I could feel it in my bones." He faced Mountalban across the desk and made his plea : " I have been faithful to music. So few have, you know. And music is of God. Perhaps—"

" You're a fool, Mr. Fitch. Death isn't as simple as that. Do you think I haven't considered the matter? It takes a long time for humanity to kick itself to death. A long time, Mr. Fitch. And it costs a lot of money. The immediate cost of the next experiment, due to take place in five minutes from now, is twenty-five million pounds. That's because they want to try a civilised form of death; and civilisation always costs a lot in the end. But they'll be quite happy with a rebate of one per cent for their Happylanders' Fund. What a figure I should cut in an expressionist play, Mr. Fitch ! I should be labelled ' God ' and the rest of the characters would bow down to me as I sat on a throne juggling with a globe spun round with gold coins."

Sweat broke out on Fitch's forehead. The room was silent, but till now there had always been the knowledge that outside the world went on making its noises. He went frantically to the window and raised it and looked out. There was no sound at all, he could hear nothing. It was like the two minutes on Remembrance Day, and he wondered if everything in the world was standing still, waiting.

"It's only your fear, Mr. Fitch. Everything is going on as usual."

But he couldn't believe it. Fear shuddered through him like fever and he returned to the chair and sat down again and saw that it was noon.

The time passed, his fear passed, his prayers for the sins of the world passed. At twelve-fifteen he felt quite his old self. "There was one other thing I had to tell you: Tom—"

"Lord," Mountalban said thinly.

"Yes. Lord Prospect is throwing half of Elysium open to Happylanders. A gesture, he calls it; a contribution to the government's rehabilitation scheme. Three months he's giving them. 'Come and taste real happiness,' he's telling them. And after the three months they can stay on if they pay—special reduced rates. There's talk of doing the same with all the Prospect camps. 'Half for Happylanders'— that's his new slogan: forced on him by the government, one might say. He has the Barony, you see. He's a man who can't resist a little vulgarity. And he thinks it's a christian gesture to show the evildoers what they've been missing, what happiness really is."

"Jollity, jollity, jollity," Mountalban murmured. He rose and went to the tape machine and read what was on the ribbon. "All very satisfactory. You'd better go home now, Mr. Fitch. Sleep for a few hours. Calm yourself. The world isn't ended after all."

Fitch went out. Relief had invested his spirit with a kind of despairing hysteria. He wanted to giggle. He had to go down in the lift because his knees were trembling so. Once in the street he found himself uncontrollably laughing. Tears sprang to his eyes and misted his glasses and he made his way toward Park Lane by feeling the railings of houses and touching the kerb with his toe. All the time he kept on laughing. Inside himself he knew it must be a dreadful sound and his inherent respectability blenched at the thought of people observing him. But he couldn't stop. He went on and reached Park Lane. He passed no-one on the way. His giggling laughter echoed thinly in the narrow street. When he reached Park Lane he saw why his journey had been solitary: the crowds were dispersing from the park, where the bunched public address loud-speakers sprouted from wire-linked poles.

The B.B.C. commentary was over. People were going back to their jobs. The buses were beginning to move slowly forward. Within his hysteria Fitch thought, ' So I was right—things *did* stop moving, there *was* a silence, there *was* a great fear. But it's all over now.'

Yes, people were moving on now. They had stopped and listened and prayed, kidding themselves it wasn't necessary but they'd better be sure, just in case. And the steady cultured tones of the commentator had gone on making little jokes about the plane and the pilot and the pilot's aim and how he hoped it was good. He stood at his observation post, wherever it was, like the centurion of Pompeii and cracked little quips about a flight of birds that flew over, and about all the trouble the Happylanders had caused, and the trouble other political systems had caused and how all the trouble would be ended from noon onward if the scientists hadn't made a gaffe. Then he went on to describe the movements of the plane again, and the movement of time, and admitted jovially to feeling a bit windy himself. Then of course he told listeners to refer to the plan in the *Radio Times*; and he began to describe exactly what would happen: how at 11.59.34 precisely the pilot would signal to his base that he was 'dead on' the target, and, by a wonderful new radar system the bomb would be released by radar, without any human intervention at all, which was a wonderful thing the scientists had dreamed up in the last month or so, and would absolutely absolve any human being from feeling guilty—because it just wouldn't be a human being at all who caused the bomb to drop, but an electronic cycle, which he hoped everybody understood because he didn't.

And at that it became 11.55 and his voice began to quiver and in a few more seconds dried up completely, so that listeners everywhere were relieved of the strain of listening to it and could concentrate on their own inmost private feelings and on straining their ears to catch the sound of the plane.

But there was no sound. The enormous silence that Fitch had felt came down over everyone. Only their hearts beat on; but those small sounds were inaudible, or perhaps stilled by fear.

Anyway, everyone was moving on now. And Fitch's laughter, the odd giggle that he would have believed himself incapable of, was in no way noteworthy. For everyone, it seemed, was a victim of the same hysteria.

By night the crowds were gathering again. It was like the celebration of peace after years of war. But the scenes throughout the country, the papers said, were unprecedented. *And rightly too. For was this strange hysteria that seized us all anything but the age-old mixture of laughter and tears that is like a vent to our relief? Was it anything but an expression of our joy that we need no longer go in fear of our lives, that from this time forward we can again time our steps to the slow and mighty march down civilisation's road to supremacy? Is there not reason enough for our joy? Should we not be proud that our scientists have given us their greastest brain-child: a weapon that can hold all the world at bay while we pursue our boundless road to peace?*

And this is now proved. Yesterday at noon the island of Happyland was targetised and immediately disintegrated, vanished as if it had never been, without noise or pain or cruelty. We could if we wanted drop a target-designated X-bomb in the centre of Moscow and cut fifty thousand square miles out of the vast land of Russia. Needless to say, we do not want. But our potential enemies have no doubt now of our capabilities. And it is this knowledge that will assure peace for us and all the future generations of the world, with the help of God, for ever-more.

A special X-bomb edition of this newspaper, made possible by the coöperation of the men who made the bomb, will be published tomorrow. It will form a worthy souvenir of a great event.

The souvenir edition was bought and glanced at and put out with the newspapers for the fishmonger. Fading in bundles with the heat of the summer sun it later mouldered in the winter's damp, until one afternoon the following year, in spring, Fitch, buying two small dabs for his Good Friday luncheon, found that they were wrapped in a copy of that same X-bomb souvenir edition.

He unfolded the damp paper and spread it on the kitchen table. They were all there—the special articles by leading men and women of the day, the advertisements for ex-Happyland indicator balloons offered at reduced prices, the long subscription lists of the Happylanders Relief Fund. The words and figures explained an event that hadn't yet assumed the sanctity of history. Fitch took the fish and laid them carefully between two plates for steaming over a saucepan. Then he crumpled the paper and threw it in the boiler. It had all happened so long ago, one was no longer interested; besides, he had a performance of the B minor Mass to attend.

He ate his luncheon slowly and carefully, peering with suspicion at each forkful of fish. When he had finished he played his record of *Frühlingsfahrt* and thought of himself as the warrior setting forth on his spring journey. When the song was ended he carefully cleared up the flat. Finally he went into the bathroom and syringed his ears so that they would serve him well at the concert. Besides, apart from the music one never knew quite what one would hear. He never really knew.

However, he heard nothing but the music. Its massive harmonies sustained him like bread and wine until, late in the evening, he called in at Cradle's and entered the smoking room, dimly aware, as he was always aware, that he had been neglectful of his duty.

The Minister was there, poised with histrionic gravity on the sofa before the fireplace; but Fitch kept to the shadows, padding toward the vacant chair on his rubber soles, sinking wearily into the leather cushions and composing himself immediately for his listening sleep. Presently the Minister was joined by a man Fitch knew to be in the Diplomatic Service. He sank down beside the Minister. " I came directly here, Minister, because it's a matter of urgency . . . perhaps gravity is the word I should use. I've come from Hecate County—"

In the mirror Fitch saw the Minister put his hand on the Diplomat's arm. " However urgent, my dear fellow, we must not discuss it here. We must go—"

The two rose and left the room. It was one of those occasions when Fitch was helpless. He must never arouse suspicion. It was the *sine qua non,* as he had often told Mountalban, never to arouse suspicion. He trusted to his hunches, always, and his genius for being in the right place at the right time. But sometimes his genius failed him. And this time the Minister, by accident or design, had foiled him. Nonetheless he had a shred of news to impart.

He left immediately and went to the Mountalban building. Hecate County: it was of course a code name, but he knew the Diplomat's normal station abroad.

Mr. Mountalban was standing by the window, a glass of wine in his hand. " Well, Mr. Fitch. You have something for me?" The wine had coloured his cheeks a little, as it might have coloured the cheeks of the simple scion of respectability whose taunting shadow had followed him always down the bleak perspectives of tumultuous finance.

Fitch wasn't breathless, but his stomach needed a re-assuring hand for a moment. " This is something grave, but I can't give you more than the gist of it—not even the gist. The parties escaped me. One cannot always . . . it's very difficult . . ."

" Few failures deserve few reproaches, Mr. Fitch. You appear too disturbed to rebuke."

"I am; O I am. And unfortunately not because of any-thing *concrete,* you understand—" Fitch's failure pricked him like a salted wound. He hadn't failed for so long. " But my intuition tells me . . . I can always tell, you know . . . anything of great gravity—it nudges me like pain. I am always certain. Even with nothing concrete to go on I am certain."

" Yes, Mr. Fitch. You've been certain many times; and always right. The idea of Happiness—"

" I was right," Fitch clutched at the thin verisimilitude of another claim and thrust it forward. In another voca-

o

tion he would have justified himself by blustering; but in this one he clung to dignity. " I was right."

Mountalban sat down. " And now?"

Fitch told him about the meeting of the Minister and the Diplomat, choosing the words ' gravity ' and ' urgency ' with the utmost care, pronouncing them as if they were in themselves possessed of the power of conviction. " Hecate County—perhaps I could find out if that name refers—"

" There will be no need, Mr. Fitch. You're only confirming news I was expecting—have been anticipating in fact." He rang for the first secretary. " Code cables to Chicago. Production schedule forty-seven; and to Oslo and Amsterdam : Plan D. I shall want Johannesburg on the telephone; they can't be trusted. Nor Essen. I shall want Dr. Isserstedt personally. For the British groups—you know what to do."

The secretary went. " Your information, vague as it is, has at least proved useful, Mr. Fitch. It might mean the earlier employment of ten thousand people."

" I don't know what it all means," Fitch said with sudden plaintiveness. " You ought to keep me informed. How else am I to know what circles require my presence as a listener; how else am I to know—"

" You know all that's necessary, Mr. Fitch. By Sunday you will know as much as everyone else."

It was true. Fitch spent Saturday in pursuit of pleasure. He allowed himself to sulk, closed his ears to everything but music. But on Sunday he read what everybody else was reading : the first whispers of a rumour that within a month was to be offered and accepted as a fact—as fact indeed it was : that another country had made for themselves an X-bomb—an altogether superior model by the use of which an area fifty times as great could be liquidated. The more serious papers referred on this Easter Sunday not to 'Z' but to Omega bombs; but by Monday it was the 'Om-bomb' that threatened the peace of the entire civilised world.

XV

THE box in which Brutus Robinson sat was raised on stilts above the Pleasure Fair. It had windows all the way round and a roof of imitation thatch. He sat on a chair in front of a console, and both chair and console revolved together at the touch of his foot on a pedal. "See," Tom Prospect's Director of Amusements had told him with juvenile enthusiasm, "you can see all round the Pleasure Fair."

"All over the island," Robinson corrected. "I can see the sea all round. The sea washing up on the sand. A God's-eye view."

"Your job's just concerned with the Pleasure Fair," the other said. "You're on Variety Div's payroll. See those luminous circles?"

The glowing rings were scattered all over the Pleasure Fair. The Director of Amusements confided, "Luminous only from up here. Down there they're invisible. Clever, eh? They mark the gratings, the ducts."

"Ducts?"

"The air-ducts. All connected with the keys on this console and the air-conditioning plant from the Telekin. Nothing wasted, see? Clever, eh? You press down one of your console keys and a blast of air pops up through the corresponding grating. All you've got to do is wait till you see a nice girl standing in a circle and then press down your key. Clever, eh? It'll cause a lot of fun down there. Pick your girls, though; and use it sparingly. I'm afraid you won't get much of a view of results yourself up here; but of course it isn't for your benefit. The customers pay— they get the views. Clever, eh?"

Robinson had been sitting in the glass-walled hut for six months now. He didn't mind the job at all, for he learned to control the keys so that girls' skirts blew really high, like inverted umbrellas, and his view from the high place was quite good. Sometimes the results of his key-pressing were most surprising and he had to release the key immediately to ensure that no complaints were made.

In the intervals of waiting for the right sort of girl to stand in the right spot (which they fairly often did deliberately, once they knew the lie of the land) he sang songs to himself or invented stories.

He saw Loomes daily in the staff dining room. Loomes was now Elysium's resident chaplain ('The Ex-Happyland Padre' the publicity proudly proclaimed) and married couples quite often in the little chapel with its stained glass windows and lilies of the valley that miraculously decorated the High Table all the year round. The marriage ceremony was performed free—' an Elysium gift."

Today, as usual, Robinson and Loomes sat opposite one another at their meal. Each of them secretly thought he saw in the eyes of the other a faint nostalgic recollection of the days of Happyland; but neither spoke of it. They were like rich people who have suddenly become impoverished: the riches of that other life, being unattainable, they quickly and sensibly (and irrevocably too, since a spell cannot be invoked but only accepted) forgot, and only sought for in each other's eyes on days when they were feeling particularly sentimental. In this they were like the rest of the Happylanders in Elysium—those to whom, in affection and awareness of their publicity value, Prospect had ordered his Welfare Division to ministrate in the specially built colony of bungies at the very edge of the island. Disenchanted, they had all quickly forgotten what it was like to know Happyland's particular happiness, and enjoyed instead the happiness of the ordinary world. Gradually they were absorbed into the life of the country and a great many of them left Elysium as soon as they got accommodation nearer their work. The Happyland affair having faded quickly from the public interest Prospect had no longer seen any particular business value in replacing those Happylanders who left by those who had been less fortunate and still sought homes and jobs. So the Happylanders Wing was at present only a third full.

" Half empty," Lord Prospect called it at the staff meeting this morning," Loomes said.

" A business drive," Robinson said. " I smell a business drive."

" It seems," Loomes said reflectively, " that a worried nation doesn't go for so many holidays. ' This is the silly season,' Lord Prospect said this morning. He said, ' The news of the Om-bomb thing has bothered the nation. They felt themselves secure and now they find they're not secure at all. They won't go for holidays while they're half expecting worse news any minute,' he said." Loomes took a morning paper from his pocket. *Foreign Ministers Conference on Om-bomb control. Hiroshima tipped as rendezvous.* " That was what he referred to. ' Leave it to the statesmen to sort things out,' he said. It seems this conference will take place next month. ' It'll quiet the nation,' he said, ' relieve the tension a bit. People are always relieved by a conference. And that's an opportunity for a publicity boost.' "

Robinson nodded. " So?"

" He's going to offer a lot of new attractions. ' It's time Happyland was dug up from public memory,' he said. So he's going to offer all ex-Happyland personnel free natal facilities during the rest of the summer. Baptisms too. He's going to board them in the empty bungies in the Happylanders Wing. ' Give 'em a chance of a get-together and a sing-song,' he said."

" We might even see someone we . . . remember," Robinson said.

He watched carefully, day by day, from his high cabin; but he saw no-one he knew. Really he was too far above the crowds to identify faces, and he wasn't allowed to possess binoculars—" In your job it wouldn't be quite decent—eh, old man?" But all the time he could see the sea washing on the shore, and because in his high small world he was remote and unconcerned and seemingly omnipotent above the crowds he felt no regret. He remembered this world from his earlier days in it. It had not altered at all. But he was a little too tired—or so it seemed—to be fiery and taunting about it any more. " We're lost," he told Loomes. He meant not only himself and Loomes but, vaguely, some vast host of people beyond comprehension.

" Yes."

One day Prospect sent for Creech. Creech came, hearty and buoyant and a little nervous. " Well, my lord—long time no see. You were right over Happyland. Didn't quite flop the way you thought, though—eh? Lord, what a national ding-dong that turned out to be. Amazing how quickly people forget though. Never hear a word about it nowadays."

"That's what I want you to do," Prospect said. He sat his cigarette in a cut-glass ashtray and stroked the head of the little dachsund. "Dig up the memory." He told Creech about his plan. "Okay?"

"Fair enough," Creech said. "There must still be plenty of those Happyland blighters kicking about. I'll set about a campaign."

"Free maternity benefits." Prospect whispered sideways to Walt Earley: "What's that word?"

"Gynaecologist."

"The best gynaecologist in England—on tap. Well, they're worth it, they're good simple people, the salt of the earth. Besides, digging up Happyland will keep people's minds off more serious things. They need a release from tension at the moment. The P.M. was saying the other day . . . but that's by the way. It's up to me to help the relief, as it were. People'll be able to face this conference, this Om-bomb do, better if they've had a load of jollity to back 'em up. So all out for all biz. Okay?"

"Sure, okay."

He watched Creech depart, wave from the speedboat that took him back to Cleethorpes. Then, flanked by Earley and Werner he made a tour of Elysium. He was recognised everywhere and waved to—there wasn't any side about him at all, he was happily conscious of it, he was a real man of the people.

Everything about the place was looking good. There was noise and laughter and jollity everywhere, the Telekin was festooned with neon, the giant racer and the dodg'ems and the centrifugal chairoplane were operating madly; and in the gardens planned by Natural Development Division there were lovers walking and whispering.

"We want a new slogan for a sign over the entrance

to Maternity Wing. Think something up, Morrie."

" Right, Tom."

" And every child that's born here and the parents stay long enough to have it baptised here an' all—I reckon we ought to give that child a christening present, a chalice or whatever it is. Something rhodium-plated. Get a quotation from some firm. And think up a saying to put on it."

" An engraved inscription," Werner said gently.

" That's the thing. Think of something good."

They walked a few steps farther round the Pleasure Fair. Werner said suddenly : " How about ' I was born in Elysium : I'm a happy Elysium child,' Tom ?"

Prospect lit a cigarette. " That's not bad. Not bad at all."

Not to be outdone, Earley said : " Why not have a flourish of trumpets to announce every child that's born ?"

" All right. But you'd best get Music Div to sort it out. Proper music I want. Classical stuff. I don't want anybody saying we haven't got taste."

" Of course not, Tom."

Creech's press campaign blossomed forth, its advertisements sandwiched between the columns of conjecture and rumour about world war, the reassuring articles by scientists and the presentation of moral problems by churchmen. The response to it was good : there were, it appeared, still many Happylanders who were dependent on public assistance and many more who were willing to pay for a holiday in Elysium for the sake of having free obstetric treatment. The Happylanders Wing filled up rapidly with its charity-tenants, and the publicity afforded this generous gesture by the newspaper columnists resulted in the camp being fully booked for the rest of the summer.

Mountalban knew of it all. He told Fitch, " You know,

Mr. Fitch, sometimes I have a great longing for a holiday—"

Fitch shook his head. " No : not I. That dreadful woman playing the Grieg! I shall never forget . . . Besides, you and I . . we're unique, creatures apart."

The two faced each other across the small walnut desk. Yes, they were enmeshed completely now; the machinations of commerce and garnered intelligence would never let them go.

Proudly, associating himself with Mountalban because he knew his own value, Fitch said : " We are like puppet-masters. People—nations—dance at our behest." With his finger alongside his bulbous nose and a bismuth tablet fizzing in a glass of water beside him he added a pleasant literary thought : " A *Danse Macabre*. Yes, a *Danse Macabre*."

Mountalban heard him go, then he himself went on up-stairs to the *Sorrows of Satan* and the infinite and hopeless longing for death.

Fitch, going slowly home to his flat, his gramophone and his ever-ready tablets and glasses of hot water, went down at the Circus and took a Piccadilly Line train; and there opposite him sat the young man from the gramophone shop—the prim but advanced Mr. Bassett (was it? the name always escaped him, it was as neutral as the man himself)—whose expressed preference was for Stravinsky and Alban Berg, but who secretly wallowed in Liszt and Tschaikowski, he was certain. And beside him his wife.

Fitch nodded bravely with friendly assurance, fighting down his embarrassment at the sight of the girl's body, and leaned across the compartment. " Allow me to congratulate you . . . I mean of course your marriage . . . I went in the shop for a little Beethoven recently and the proprietor told me . . ." He felt the embarrassment troubling his stomach and wished he hadn't spoken. They looked so woodenly at him, embarrassed themselves, he supposed. " You're off on a journey?"

Harold Bassett nodded. He had discarded the hat and the pipe; his hair was glossily Brylcreamed now and a cigarette stained his fingers. " Taking the wife to a nursing-home up north." He had changed. *Transcendental* and dry Martinis and the longing to absolve Doris from sentimentality had gone with the hat. He was back where he belonged, he was home again. His own family and the Cheesmans had seen them off, the mothers' tiny handkerchiefs were sodden, the fathers' handshakes were firm. It was all all right. " Back into our lives," Mrs. Bassett had said with glistening eyes. " To comfort our declining days." And his father had drunk a toast in ginger wine—it was the Buffalo toast: " May you ever climb the hills of prosperity and never meet a brother coming down." The sticky wine had coloured Mr. Bassett's pale lips and he'd said: " When you come back, boy, we'll have you inducted. I can get you in my lodge."

" Up north?" Fitch said. " Elysium, no doubt." It was Holborn. He rose. " Well, believe me, I do wish you every happiness." Coyly he put his hand on Doris's shoulder. " And what is it to be—the little one?" But he had no time to wait for an answer. He waved from the platform as the train drew away, but the two of them sat rigid as wooden models, not even turning to acknowledge him.

" Cheeky old devil," Harold said. With the hand that held the cigarette he offered Doris a reassuring gesture— just a touch on the arm, but it thrilled her. " Oh Hal— you're such a dear, nice person, a proper Galerad."

" Gala—" but his corrections never came to anything nowadays; he accepted Doris as she was, faults and all. She needed comforting just now.

" Anyway, he wished us happiness—dear old boy."

" And happiness is what we're going to have—lashings of it. The real stuff this time." A flickering memory of Happyland crossed his mind and he prodded at it scornfully. " None of that fantastic stuff."

At King's Cross he herded her carefully into the train and stored the suitcase and the anticipatory folded Karricot on the rack; and when the journey was ended and they entered Elysium his hand was at her elbow. It was a gesture he couldn't repudiate.

Pleasure Fair, the brightly painted signposts said. *Maternity Wing, Bungies, Romantic Wilderness.* There was no fear of confusion.

" Organisation," he said with proprietorial pride. " That's what you get in these places."

And you're kept in touch with the world too. The loudspeakers relayed the news and every edition of the newspapers was on sale at the Emporium of Literature. People took an interest too: everyone you met had an opinion on world affairs.

" I tell you, they'll never use no Om-bomb. Stands to reason. If they did—"

" Wipe the swine out before they get the chance—"

" What I say is, it isn't christian—"

" Of course there's an answer. There's an antidote to every poison—"

" Time. We want time to prepare. Why don't our blokes get cracking, make a bigger bomb still? Time—"

Time moved inexorably on. They had been in Elysium a week when the clinic doctor ordered Doris to take her place in the Maternity Wing. " He thinks it'll be tonight. they've got a lovely idea, Hal. It's to stop fathers hanging about the wing and getting in the way. They announce the birth of every baby with music over the loudspeakers.

' Fanfare for a Newborn Babe.' they call it. Specially composed for Elysium it was. I think it's ever such a nice idea."

He left her. It was then midday, oppressively hot, with sun-lined clouds bulging tumultuously across the sky. He ate his meal in the bunting-hung communal dining hall. He felt no anxiety at all as yet and a glossy pride at his own calmness stirred in him. ' She'll be all right.' The doctors never failed and the best gynaecologist in England was in attendance. And anyway it wouldn't be before night.

In the afternoon he toured the Pleasure Fair. Years of suppressed longing for jollity had made him eager. He tried everything with juvenile enthusiasm. The shrieks from the switchbacks and chairoplanes merged with the roundabout's steady rhapsody. *Jollity, jollity—All is Jollity* a sign read. Harold Bassett paused with a thick ice-cream wafer in his hand and watched a girl's skirt blow high as she turned a corner. " A bit of all right," the man next to him nudged. He had an eye for leg and dainties himself. The ice-cream smudged his chin a little. " Yes."

" Looks like a storm coming up. One thing about this place, you can escape, there's always somewhere to go."

He chose the cinema as the storm broke. When he came out it had cleared, the canvas and bunting were steaming in the sun; but the sea had not abated, its enormous thundering could be heard as the roundabout stopped and the switchback car came to rest at the end of each journey. In the Romantic Wilderness the sea was louder still in the stillness of arbours and lovers' nooks. He left there and returned to his bungalow and ate the sandwich tea he had bought at the Olde Tucke Shoppe. Still he felt no anxiety : only a certainty that everything would be all right, a sense of achievement, and a mild desire to visit the Pleasure Fair again and watch the girls' windblown skirts.

This he did. On the way there he heard the loudspeakers spurt out their news. " Conference," they said. " Om-bomb control conference fails. Cabinet to . . . Urgent defence measures . . . Recall of . " Most of it was lost as the switchback car started on another journey and the women began to scream. He shrugged, said to a man next to him in the queue for newspapers : " They'll start another one —conference, I mean. They always do." Happily he nudged : " Anyway, I've got something better to think about. I'm about to become a father. The trumpets'll sound any minute now."

He turned, seeing the familiar bulbous nose, the stuck-out ears, the embodiment of silent listening.

" I told him," Fitch said with satisfaction. " I told him long, long ago. Erosion, you know, the end of it all; the place being washed away. My little intuitions are always right. And I've just heard it confirmed. I'm returning to London now, to Mr. Mountalban. ' I told you so,' I shall say." With his finger to his lips he stole away on his rubber soles, was gone, lost amid the jollity.

Again Harold Bassett shrugged, went with his news-paper past the Novelty Shoppe, halted and bought a joke inkstain and a packet of itching powder and a cornucopia of candyfloss. The devilment of youth possessed him and he sang suddenly as if for the last time, aloud : " Whoopee ! Whoopee !"—thinking as he watched the girls, ' Old fool. He crops up everywhere. What the hell does he mean, the end of it all?'

But it didn't matter. He tried the Dodg'ems and the Disc of Death and the Target for Tonight, where he won tenpence. He tried everything and by that time it was dusk. His lapels were sticky with candyfloss as he came off the roundabout for the last time. Its cacophony wheezed to silence behind him and he stood shrieking " Whoopee! Whoopee!" as above the dying wail of jollity he heard the trumpets flare out in their immense and brassy triumph.